THAT DAY

A STORY OF NATIONAL SURVIVAL

DWIGHT BECHTEL

Outskirts Press, Inc.
Denver, Colorado

That Day
A Story of National Survival

Information available at WWW.ARMY.MIL is consistent with Army and DoD policies and The Principles of Information and contains information cleared for public release. Information intended for the internal Army audience is available through Army Knowledge Online (AKO) at www.us.army.mil

Outskirts Press
http://www.outskirtspress.com

ISBN-10: 1-4327-0393-5
ISBN-13: 978-1-4327-0393-6

Outskirts Press and the "OP" logo are trademarks belonging to Outskirts Press, Inc.

Printed in the United States of America

DEDICATION

This book is dedicated to all those Americans who have sacrificed their lives and limbs for the freedoms to which we have become accustomed. Further, it is dedicated to those who have suffered at the hands of the greedy and the immoral people who occupy the seats of power in this country. We have long stood at the crossroads between a wicked and immoral world and a free society. Our soldiers and others have sacrificed their lives that we might have a Christian nation where everyone may worship or not worship at all as they please. No religious zealot has ever been permitted to exercise control over this nation. They have tried, but failed. In the latter times we have been confronted by a minority who want to eliminate Christianity from our nation. I pray that we will fight just as hard to stop these people from dictating to our country. I also pray that the events depicted in this novel will never occur.

TABLE OF CONTENTS

FOREWORD

Time: A time in the future.

Situation: The war in Iraq had dragged on for many years, and neither political party had brought about an end. Because of political pressure, the draft had not been re-instituted. The military strength of America had dwindled to numbers which were alarming. The National Guard had been unable to enlist sufficient numbers since being called upon to serve in a foreign war. Petroleum prices are out of sight. The citizens were outraged at the prices for fuel. Particularly annoying were the home heating bills for the past winter. It was a very trying time for the U.S.

North Korea was still negotiating their nuclear power program. China seemed to offer no real help in the negotiations. Several analysts believed that North Korea had sold both missiles and nuclear warheads to some Mideast countries. Some thought that the missiles were being smuggled through China (along the old trade routes). If so they were doing it by Yak drawn wagons, because our satellites would have detected any large motor drawn vehicles. Still, there had been some activity along the old trade routes. A better bet was that the oil tankers and/or cargo ships were transporting missiles and warheads.

Additionally, China had built up its military forces to a number that was surprising among Western analysts. The most articulated number was one hundred million in uniform. China made statements that the forces were needed to calm the population, after a few years of below expectations of crops. In some parts of China people were having trouble getting enough to eat. The leaders of China looked at the productive crops of South America as a way to avoid starvation for their people. And China had made some investments in those countries. Underneath the feelings of many was that China had put strong arm pressure on Brazil and Chile to send more food. But, of course, the United States was a stumbling block in that effort. Russia had also become alarmed at the build up of China's Army, and the new nuclear submarines.

CHAPTER 1
A STORY BEFORE THAT DAY

fter working in the oil fields of Iran for three years, Joe and Rita Richardson decided to take the tanker Esfahan, as passengers, from Bandar-e 'Abbas, Iran off the Strait of Hormez to Hong Kong. (Although the final destination for the ship was Shanghai, China.) From Hong Kong they planned to fly home to Springfield, Missouri. The idea was to take some time to write about their experiences among the hospitable peoples of western Iran. They knew that it would be hard to write after arriving home. There would be continuous family and friends to deal with, plus a job. So for now it seemed like a good idea to take a leisurely drawn out cruise. The tanker was well equipped with exercise equipment, a good chef, comfortable rooms and connections to satellites for communications.

So, on October 7, **That Day** minus two years and five months the tanker Esfahan departed Iran, with 35 crew members, Joe, Rita and two other male passengers, Adou Barak and Killen

Dabou who were dressed in traditional garments. The crew was made up of 22 Iranians, three Saudis, four Turks, two Afghans, and four Indonesians. The particular makeup of the crew by nationality did not seem important at the beginning of the trip. Later it would draw great significance for Joe and Rita. The tanker was equipped with guns fore, aft and one on each side in the middle of the ship. One day Captain Arn Salim explained about the guns, "These are not for protection from anyone's navy, but for protection from the scavengers of the sea. How do you call them?" Joe replied, "Pirates?" Captain Arn continued, "Yes, that's it. Sometimes they have been known to come alongside with guns, board the ship, and rob the crew. They only do this where there are many islands around for them to escape into them. Tomorrow we will have some practice firing the guns. The gunners really look forward to their turn at firing some really heavy guns. So be prepared."

The trip to Hong Kong would take about a month. The cruising speed was about 12 knots and it was a long journey, some 4400 nautical miles, although parts of the journey prohibited the 12 knot speed. Also the tanker would anchor off Singapore for one day and take on fresh supplies. The crew was pleasant enough. Captain Arn was very friendly and seemed pleased to find that Joe was a decent chess player. They played nearly every day, until almost a week into the trip. The ship was south of India at the time.

On the 5th day, October 12th, there was a good deal of disturbance among the crew. The cabin attendant, John Abraham, came by and explained, "The three Saudis have disappeared. No one can find them. The Captain thinks that they have fallen overboard. It is very scary, because all three have been on many trips with Captain Salim." Captain Arn seemed very distressed over the issue. Safety was a major concern and the three would be missed.

Captain Arn explained at dinner that night, "Two of the Saudis were skilled communications officers. Their absence leaves our ship with only one communications officer. The three have been arguing about religion and technical aspects of the digital communications procedures. Maybe the arguments became violent and they ended up dragging each other over the railings and into the sea. I just don't know!

"I have asked other members of the crew if they heard anything, but so far, I have no additional information. There was some blood near the railings just to the aft of the communications center. I will report the incident to the authorities in Hong Kong and back to Iran. Meanwhile, please exercise some caution."

From that day to the end of the journey, the

entire crew seemed to be on edge. Tempers flared often. This was not going to be the pleasant cruise that Joe and Rita had anticipated. After this Adou Barak and Killen Dabou rarely spoke to Joe and Rita, and the Captain was rarely available for chess.

Three days later, John (the cabin attendant) came to their cabin very excited, "Rallou and Gahr, the two Afgan deck hands have disappeared. They were good workers. I'm afraid. What's happening? Please don't tell the Captain that I told you!"

Now Joe and Rita were really worried.

October 17th the ship was negotiating the Strait of Malacca and the scenery was breathtaking. The tanker anchored near Singapore in the early evening of the 18th. The next day Joe and Rita hopped on board the supply shuttle for a day in Singapore. The day was a magnificent whirl of a tourist barge, lunch at the 'Hawker Centre' street kitchens, a quick trip on the underground mass transit system, a view of the very modern downtown skyscrapers, and a rickshaw ride back to the dock by the 6:00 p.m. departure time.

On October 20 while straightening their room, John blurted out, "The four Turks did not return to the ship yesterday. Two of them worked in the engine room. I don't know how we will manage without them. Please be very careful around the ship." Five days later in the Sea of China, the four

Indonesians disappeared. Nothing was said to Joe and Rita, but they no longer showed up for any meals. Joe and Rita began to fear for their own lives. Writing about their experiences in Iran became untenable. They stayed in their cabin whenever possible and never let each other out of sight. They were very suspicious of the two mysterious passengers. What were they up to. Joe and Rita began discussing the possible reasons for the disappearances. Joe stated, "Maybe there are religious differences." But Rita countered, "There has been no discussion about religion among the crew, but several of the crew do bow toward Mecca three times a day. The bowing seems to be evenly distributed among the different nationalities on board. I don't believe that could be the reason."

Joe said, "Well, something is going on. I'm not sure that we are safe. Is there any way to get off this ship?"

Rita answered, "You know as well as I do that the next port is Hong Kong. We could pretend to be sick and get a helicopter to take us somewhere. Maybe to Manilla?"

Joe thought a minute, then said, "I believe that would make them very suspicious of us. Let's just stick it out to Hong Kong."

The crew was now comprised of only Iranians! What really bothered the two was the lack of any kind of on board investigation into the disappearances. It was as if it was expected. If

Joe and Rita were thrown overboard, would the event be treated the same way? Were they in danger?

Finally, on November 4, the Esfahan entered the bay area around Hong Kong, and docked near Kowloon. Joe and Rita gathered their belongings and were able to catch a sea taxi into Hong Kong. They were required to do the usual customs inspection routine, which lasted until darkness had started to settle in. The sea taxi operator suggested the Guangdong Hotel in the heart of Tsim Sha Tsui in Kow-loon district, close to main tourist attractions and shopping centers. Out of customs, they took a cab to the hotel. When they finally registered and arrived in their room, they just relaxed. The room was on the twelfth floor with a nice view of the Kow-loon district, but Joe and Rita were only interested in collapsing into their beds. They had never felt so exhausted in their entire lives.

When they awakened the next day it was almost noon, but they didn't care. After cleaning up and finding something to eat it was 2:30. Next they caught a cab to the American embassy. While in the cab the driver mentioned that there appeared to be a vehicle following them. Rita thought, "Will this nightmare never stop!"

Inside the embassy they told their preliminary story to a clerk, who ushered them into a small office. They sat there about an hour, until they became frustrated with the situation, and started to leave. As they got up to make their way out, in came a young American woman, Ms. Jenkins. She apologized for the delay, but explained that she was helping a group from Mississippi. It had taken longer than she expected.

As Joe and Rita started explaining all that had happened they came to the first disappearances, Ms. Jenkins stopped them. "Wait here for a moment, please. This is out of my job description. I'll have to get someone else to aid you."

Some minutes passed, and Ms. Jenkins returned. She ushered them into another room. From the looks of the room, Joe and Rita assumed that it was a secure room – no windows, and several security cameras could be seen. Both were further alarmed. At that moment, a rather large gentleman of obvious Asian descent came in. He introduced himself in excellent American English as Hank Williams, and laughed a little. His name had been given to him by his Chinese mother and Tennessee father. He apologized for the delay, but got right down to asking questions. As best they could, Joe and Rita went over the entire trip.

At the end, some three hours later, Hank advised them, "Don't tell this story to anyone else. I don't think that you are in any danger, but my best advice is to leave for the United States as quickly as possible."

Joe and Rita grabbed a taxi to a small

traditional Chinese restaurant, and had a relaxing meal. By the time they had finished their meal, it was after 9:00 p.m. When they got up to leave, a man from another table appeared to get up immediately and headed to the exit. They caught a cab and now both were looking back to see if they were being followed. Sure enough another car followed them very closely back to the hotel. When Joe and Rita arrived back at the Guangdong Hotel, they found that there luggage had been thoroughly searched. "What was going on?", they thought. They went immediately to the phone and got in touch with the airlines. They scheduled the first flight that would take them back to the States. That would be almost twenty-four hours later. There was a Northwest flight direct to Seattle. Thank Goodness!

Three days later Joe and Rita were back in Springfield. Upon arriving home (after more than three years) they were greeted by some friends at the airport, and taken to their home where they met the house sitter, who had gotten the house into excellent shape for them. Joe said to Rita, "How wonderful to be home. And do we have some tales to tell our friends and family."

But the next morning, an FBI agent came calling. Agent Warren 'Curly' Harper came to the door, "May I come in? We have some things to talk about." Joe came to the door, "May I see some identification?" Curly showed his I.D. Joe responded, "Please allow me to check this out." He scribbled down his I.D. number and went to the phone.

Joe turned to Rita, "Would you look up the number for the FBI?" In a couple of minutes Rita called out, "555-1234".

When Joe got the operator at the FBI office, he stated, "An agent Warren 'Curly' Harper is at our door. His I.D. is XXXXXXXXX. Can you describe this agent to me?" The operator said, "One moment please."

A voice at the other end spoke briskly, "This is agent Cody Lester, how may I help you?" Joe repeated the question. Agent Cody Lester answered, "He is about 6'1", heavyset, 35 years old, blonde hair and beginning to bald." Joe said, "Thank you. I believe that is him at out door right now."

Curly proceeded, "We understand that you had some problems on board a ship. A tanker out of Iran, I believe." Rita responded, "Actually we didn't personally have a problem, but there were some strange occurrences on board."

Curly asked, "Just for verification would you please relate all that happened?"

So Joe and Rita went over the details once more. Curly stated, "If you remember anything else about your trip, please get in touch with me. I will always try to be available."

When he left, Joe and Rita talked about all that had happened, and did they really have to be quiet about the events. They decided that they would say nothing for a while and see if anything other strange events occurred. Nothing did for the next two years, and they gradually began talking to their friends and relatives about all that had happened to them.

CHAPTER 2
THE SAILING VESSELS

Eureka, California: It was little noticed at the time, but a small number of sleek sailing vessels entered the harbor in Eureka, California on March the 10th at just before dusk. No one called the Coast Guard, nor notified the local police. The ships docked almost without notice. One old sea dog, who always stayed close to the docks after retirement, did notice that all of the sailors appeared oriental. They all had loose clothing and seemed to stay in small clusters. Otherwise, nothing seemed strange. Anyway they only seemed to want some fuel and food supplies. They would obviously be on their way in a short while. Probably they would spend the night on their ships, and be on their way by daybreak.

Sure enough the little sailing vessels were on their way at daybreak, except for one that appeared to have a broken mast.

Brunswick, Georgia: The small sailing ships moved easily between St. Simon's and Jekyll

Island and sought the safety of the harbor. Obviously they were looking for a safe harbor after a small storm had stirred the Atlantic Ocean during the day. The only strange thing about these ships was that they were all identical. "Some sort of club," observed Harry Blank, a long term resident. They also sought only fuel and food. Very innocuous. Still the ships were not like the others scattered around the harbor. Also the sailors were all dark skinned, but not African-American. Harry thought it was strange, but he had other problems to solve, and so went about his business. Anyway it was the business of the Coast Guard to check out such things. However, the Coast Guard had been extremely busy with a report from several fishermen that a submarine had collided with one of their boats. The Coast Guard sent both a rescue ship and a helicopter to help out, but found no evidence of any sub. But subs were common to these waters since the Navy had installed that base at St. Mary's just down the coast. Tomorrow the Coast Guard would check with the Navy.

Sure enough the little sailing vessels were on their way at daybreak, except for one that appeared to have a broken mast. Historians recorded this location as a mistake. They believed that the men manning the sailing vessels had intended to leave the disabled boat at St. Mary's near the Sub base.

In later times, it would be noted that similar

happenings must have occurred at small harbors from the Gulf of Mexico to Maine and up and down the West Coast. All were seemingly harmless at the time. Historians would note that such data was supposed to be accumulated at the Office of the Homeland Security in Washington.

March 11, 8:00 a.m.: In Jersey City, New Jersey, across the Hudson River from the southern tip of the island of Manhattan, N.Y. among the stacks of containers, a high level of radiation was detected. This was immediately communicated to Washington, and the area was evacuated. The inspectors waited for word from Washington, where the Director of Homeland Security, John Taylor, was notified. John was a retired general from the Marine Corps. John was all business, and interrupted his morning jog upon receiving the message. He immediately demanded that the inspectors don anti radiation clothing and go isolate the container. In Jersey City the inspectors scratched their heads. They had no such gear. A request had been made for such clothing, but had bogged down in a budget battle in Congress. No one wanted to go near the radiation area. The Atomic Energy Commission was contacted for help. Three Mile Island was the nearest nuclear plant with appropriate clothing. John Taylor directed a helicopter from the FBI to go after the clothing, but this would take most of the day. He tried Newport, Rhode Island, Navy base – success. A navy helicopter could have the suits to Jersey City in just two hours about 11:00 a.m.

In the Far East, the monitoring systems in Taiwan detected a lot of activity toward the mainland of China, and this was reported to the Pentagon. In Israel two bombs had exploded earlier in the day, with no loss of life. North Korea massed troops at the DMZ.

CHAPTER 3
WHAT'S HAPPENING

March 11, 20XX Springfield, Missouri (Springfield - Branson Regional Airport)

Joe and Rita Richardson are at the Springfield airport, waiting to board a plane for a long overdue Caribbean cruise. The plane is due to depart at 10:45 a.m. CST. The Richardsons arrive early for the flight to Memphis, and the connection to Ft. Lauderdale. It is now 9:45 a.m. While waiting in line to check their luggage, they feel a distant rumble. Just after checking their luggage they sit near a television set. Suddenly Joe says, "Look at that

cloud back toward Kansas City. It looks just like a mushroom cloud from an atomic bomb." Then the TV starts talking about some kind of emergency. Rita says, "Surely that won't affect our trip. What could reach all the way down here." Rita couldn't be more wrong.

First they flash a message that their flight is going to be late, then about noon they see a B2 bomber landing, and shortly after that, a cargo plane lands, and begins to taxi towards the control tower. What they see next is unbelievable. Some troops start unloading off the cargo plane and the B2 turns and fires a missile at the cargo plane. The cargo plane goes up in an explosion and a cloud of smoke. Police and National Guard troops are out shooting at the troops who survived the explosion. It all happens so quickly that Joe cannot quite take it in. He wonders, "Is this some sort of movie set?" Rita says, "Maybe we ought to look at the news on the TV." **That Day** had arrived.

Gradually the news pours in. First Kansas City has been blown up, then St Louis has also suffered a nuclear attack, along with Whiteman AFB, Missouri, the B2 Air Base. Joe and Rita return home as fast as possible. They don't realize that they have been witnesses to a lot of what is now happening. Their world will never be the same. Leisurely cruises have suddenly become a way of the past. Meanwhile, they ask, "What can we do to help?" The answer comes the next day, as thousands of injured and radiation poisoned people show up in Springfield. They must be cared for. Joe and Rita become caretakers for two families. One father was in Kansas City and is presumed dead, the other mother suffered the same fate. All the rest have suffered from some level of radiation poisoning.

The next month becomes a struggle to get food, medical supplies, and clean water. They join the rest of America in the daily struggle to just stay alive. The prayer becomes, "Give us this day our daily bread." Joe and Rita had never really had to pray this prayer. Food and shelter had always been there. Could they survive this?

CHAPTER 4

THAT DAY: THE ATTACK 11:00 AM EST, MARCH 11

It all happened without warning. Fifty-two nuclear and thermonuclear[1] weapons detonated without even a hint of notification. Jersey City, New Jersey, was obliterated along with parts of Manhattan, Brooklyn and Newark, New Jersey. Coastal cities, small and large, and inland cities of Chicago, St. Louis, Cincinnati, Detroit, Kansas City, Dallas, Minneapolis-St. Paul, Pittsburgh, Philadelphia, Phoenix, Indianapolis and Cleveland were gone or severely damaged. The only large cities of more than two million inhabitants left unharmed were Atlanta, Denver, and miraculously – Washington, D.C. Days later a bomb was located along the Potomac on a barge loaded with shipping containers. The denoting device had failed. Also in Eureka, California and Brunswick, Georgia, the two small sailing vessels had left thermonuclear weapons

---

[1] Nuclear = atomic, Thermonuclear = hydrogen

which had failed to detonate. On the Mississippi River about 30 miles south of Memphis a bomb had exploded, and caused only minor damage to the Bluff City, but destroyed the gambling casinos of Tunica, Mississippi.

It was appalling. Where had all these bombs come from and how did they get here? Early estimates put the fatalities between 50 and 100 million, and that many more needing medical care, but most large city hospitals were destroyed.

President Jake Oderon scrambled to his helicopter and headed for deep cover in Colorado, but there was no Air Force One. Even though Washington had been missed in the attack, nearby Andrews Air Force base had been nuked. The President went to Yeager Airport in Charleston, West Virginia. There he was met by an Air National Guard C-5 from Memphis, Tennessee.

Then he proceeded to Colorado Springs, Colorado. Deep in the mountains he directed the counter attack. But first there was the question of where had these bombs come from? The answer was not long in coming. From the tankers waiting to unload their cargo, a new menace came. The ships were not hauling crude oil. They were hauling troops, and missiles. The first missiles were aimed at the military bases. Every military base in Florida, California, and Texas was either destroyed or badly crippled. Newport News, Virginia and surrounding areas were gone. Ft. Dix, New Jersey was barely missed, but McGuire Air Force Base sustained major damage and radiation. The runways at the Base were unusable, and most of the aircraft were damaged. New London, Rhode Island, was gone, along with the naval base. Ft. Bragg, North Carolina, was gone. Within hours all but a few of our military bases lay in ruins. It was obviously an attempt to rapidly destroy our ability to strike back.

The National Guard was called into action. The Coast Guard was directed to stop and search all vessels in American waters.

It was suspected that China had provided the weapons, Venezuela, and Middle East groups provided the tankers, and China had sufficient submarines to cause damage to some bases. Then the tankers began disgorging their supplies of men and arms. Landing craft were dispatched to cities such as Mobile, Alabama, Ft. Lauderdale, Florida, Wilmington, Delaware, and Corpus Christie, Texas. Some were from Cuba, but most were obviously Chinese. They spread across these four cities rapidly and effectively established beachheads in the four lightly guarded cities. Many citizens were killed as they fought back with hunting rifles, shotguns and handguns.

On the West coast the towns of Coos Bay and Northbend, Oregon and Monterey, California, were chosen as appropriate beachheads.

It would be forever remembered as **That Day**.

In the early evening, President Oderon spoke to the nation. Here are a few excerpts from that memorable speech.

"Fellow Americans, we have been attacked by an assailant from a foreign land who has no regard for human life. Millions have perished. The attack was completely unprovoked. The only reason for these attacks is for world domination by an evil empire. They have attacked us by using the very openness of our society. The nuclear weapons were smuggled into our country, and detonated for the very purpose of leaving us helpless. Helpless? We are not helpless!! We have dispatched missiles and submarines to rain down on our enemies. Over the next few days you may be bewildered by attacks on our soil, in some cities, and against our military bases. But in the end we will prevail. Make no mistake about it. We will fight them in the streets, in our rivers, on our coasts, in the sea, and in their homelands. They will be brought to a sorry end.

Meanwhile, for those of you who were near sites of nuclear explosions, please take cover until such time as officials can make it known to you that the air and ground are safe to use.

This I ask of every citizen, please pray for our country and the rest of the free world. May God put our enemies to flight."

CHAPTER 5
ONE SUCCESS : MARCH 11 (THAT DAY)

George Ware and his wife Emerald woke up as usual this bright and warm day in early March. The three boys, Jonathan, twelve, Jared, nine, and Joseph, seven, ate a hearty breakfast, fussed about school work, but went to school as usual. Yesterday, Jonathon came in announcing, "Dad, guess what." George answered with the customary, "What?" (It is a strange thing in our language that we know better than to really guess what. I guess a stranger to our country might have responded with, "Did you make all A's this six weeks?") Anyway Jonathon continued, "I'm getting to try out with the baseball team." George replied, "That's wonderful son. I really hope you make it. If you do, I will try to get to as many games as I can. When are the tryouts?" Jonathon excitedly responded, "Tomorrow."

Then Jared and Joseph had to join in with something special. Jared shouted, "I got a 100 on my spelling test yesterday." George gave a shrug and said,"Wonderful, Jared." Joseph hollered, "Dad, my teacher said I was one of the best readers in my class." Another shrug and George replied, "That's great Joseph." Each boy received a hug in turn.

As George departed for work, he looked at Emerald (his wife), "The boys are really growing up. I love you." Then off to his job at the warehouse, where he was the foreman for the last three years. Nothing seemed out of the ordinary in Eugene, Oregon, this morning. But George Ware was a captain in the National Guard, having served in combat zones twice since enlisting in the Army just out of high school. While in the Army he saved in the education funds as much as he was allowed. Later, he used the tuition and living expense money to attend Oregon State University where he met and married Emerald, whose eyes matched her name. They settled near her childhood home in Eugene. While at Oregon State he had entered the ROTC, and earned a commission in the Army National Guard. Twice he had been called to active duty and served in Afghanistan both times. He had seen friends killed and had earned several medals for heroism and a purple heart after being wounded while on patrol.

At 8:00 a.m., PST, that fateful morning, the blast from the bomb that was detonated in Portland, was felt in Eugene. Then came the news. At first it told very little about what had happened. All the initial reports were saying was that Portland had been blown up. It appeared to be a nuclear blast, but no one knew for sure. By 11:00 a.m. there were additional reports about other cities such as San Francisco, and Seattle being bombed. School was dismissed early. The President had ordered all National Guard and Reservists to report to the nearest military post or armory. George excused himself from work and headed to the National Guard Armory. There he found himself to be the ranking officer. All his superiors were in Portland for a meeting. By 3:00 p.m. it was clear that, probably, they were all dead. He quickly ordered his men to make a quick rundown of the available equipment and condition of both it and the men. Then he ordered everyone to return home and show up tomorrow at 6:00 a.m. ready for action.

In addition he asked the local clergy to be there.

That fateful morning George bid his family goodbye. He had no idea where his unit would be sent, nor how soon, nor how long. It was a frightful scene.

The next morning, March 12, Captain George Ware of the National Guard was made aware of the invasion force at Coos Bay. He then realized that he and his soldiers, along with any reserves he could round up, were the most important defense for the state, maybe even the United States. Although the Guard was undermanned, he determined to do all he could. Fortunately, his unit had returned from overseas duty only five months before. Others from surrounding communities showed up. Whatever equipment they had would have to do. So with ten tanks and a number of shoulder launched missiles, he unloaded the armory, and headed for Coos Bay. With Marine and Army reserves and a few Sailors they set out, with the presumption that they would never see home again. They numbered only 1,202 men and women, some with no battle experience. But before beginning their fateful journey, he asked for prayers, knowing that only God could spare them from an almost certain destiny with death. Several protestant ministers, one Catholic priest and one rabbi prayed for the men and women.

On March 13, they spotted the first infiltrators near Elkton. Quickly they hid everything they had in garages, houses, shopping centers, and canyons. Then the best trained hand to hand combat soldiers were sent out to kill the advance party. Because of the surprise, the deeds were carried out with extreme efficiency. Not one enemy soldier was able to transmit a message.

Then a drone came overhead. Everything was sufficiently hidden. The enemy was not expecting any substantial resistance this early in the invasion.

By a huge stroke of luck a military satellite was passing over, and it was just the communication device that the small band of soldiers needed. A link was set up with Colorado.

From there it was determined that the Air National Guard base just outside Portland, was barely damaged. Quickly air support was requested, and granted. The base had some older F-15s which would provide an air strike against the advancing Chinese force. But the Air Guard needed some ground information. Captain Ware immediately sent out some patrols to determine the size and locations of the enemy. Extreme cover was needed for a successful reconnaissance. Radio silence, except for satellite communications, was in force.

A welcome fog rolled in from the Pacific. Visibility was limited to about 200 yards. Sergeant Williams, and Lance Corporal George led the two units, both of whom were battled hardened veterans. Near Scottsburg, Sergeant Williams encountered a large force. Concealing themselves between the trees and along the river, they called in the first strike against a surprised enemy. The Chinese were so sure of the success of the surprise attack that they weren't even trying to hide. Also, the Chinese were a little slow in arming their own missiles. The Chinese were only able to launch a single heat-seeking missile against the F15s. The missile did not strike its target. The F15s bore in with surprising accuracy. The Chinese were so confused that several of the soldiers fled directly toward Sgt. Williams patrol, which now let loose with everything they had. During the ensuing battle, the Chinese were almost totally wiped out. The remaining few surrendered. It was the first victory for America in the first land battle on American soil since the Indian Wars and the first against a foreign foe since the Mexican War.

Lance Cpl. George did not fare as well. He had gone down the Interstate to Green, to circle down highway 42. In Winston he met the enemy, and also called in the air strike, Before the strike could be engaged, the Chinese spotted his patrol, and after a furious firefight, the entire patrol was wiped out. But the Air Guard did inflict severe losses on the Chinese unit. Now Cpt. Ware and his tanks and men advanced toward Roseburg, and there met the enemy. The Chinese were armed primarily with small missiles, and for transportation – commandeered cars and trucks. They were no match for the ten tanks and group of trained soldiers, fighting as if there was no tomorrow.

Cpt. Ware transmitted back to Colorado the results of the battle. Twenty of his men were killed and he lost two tanks. There were more than 1,500 dead Chinese and another 90 were being held captive. The celebration at the underground facility was unbelievable. However, everyone knew that this was only a small victory, in a devastating attack on America. Even where the enemy had not struck, people would soon be running out of food and water. The situation was desperate. How could America fight a well-equipped enemy, and at the same time provide for its own citizens?

CHAPTER 6
KOREA, MARCH 11

The North Koreans launched an attack on the South. Missiles came first. The first were aimed at Seoul, Osan Air Force Base, and Korean military bases in Pusan, but the North did not have sufficient information to attack the main South Korean bases located in camouflaged places across the country. But our Patriot Antimissile systems were very effective. Some did detonate over South Korean soil, but the Patriots did their deadly work by killing most of the north Korean missiles (Scuds).

Then the Americans and South Koreans went into action. The available missiles from old stockpiles (manned by American troops) rained down on North Korea. Some of the nuclear weapons were more than 40 years old. Several had deteriorated and failed to explode. But those that did stopped North Korean forces and destroyed the nuclear facilities and the capital of Pyongyang. The South Koreans highly motivated and trained forces crossed the DMZ with startling speed. North Korean forces surrendered in vast numbers. They were simply not willing to fight for the leaders who had treated the population with such hardships for more than seventy years. The Chinese were too busy with the attack on America, to bother helping North Korea. The South Korean Air Force won a similar victory in the air, with the aid of American planes based in Korea and Japan.

March 12: The South Koreans realized that the North Korean soldiers were no threat to the south and quickly invited all who were willing to fight with the South to ward off any attack by China. Evidently China had not foreseen such a development, and had no substantial force ready to invade Korea.

The American forces, who remained in South Korea, followed the Korean forces into the North, and planned the strategies for a land-based attack on China.

North Korea did manage to launch one nuclear tipped missile toward Japan, but it exploded near Sado in the Sea of Japan. There was no significant damage to the Japanese Islands.

Korea was no longer a problem, but the United States had lost two of its most important bases in the Far East: The Eighth Army Headquarters in Seoul and Osan Air Force Base. Both were damaged severely with almost all personnel dead. Since the Eighth Army Headquarters was adjacent to Seoul, Korean fatalities were also very high. Later estimates were: 875,000 civilians killed from the three nuclear explosions. **That Day** would be forever remembered as the most tragic day in the history of Korea, but at the same time, the day that united North and South Korea.

CHAPTER 7
MOBILE, ALABAMA, MARCH 12

In Mobile, Alabama, the tanker Esfahan sailed into Mobile Bay. Landing craft with troops began their deadly excursion into Mobile. A small contingent of police and National Guard quickly converged at the waterfront, but the Chinese were armed with modern missiles and automatic weapons. The police and guard were completely overwhelmed. Mobile was in the hands of an enemy for the first time since the War Between the States. Also the force spread out to attack the Airport, but the main force remained at Mobile Bay. The airport had not fallen into Chinese hands yet.

Maj. General H. C. Hamilton, commander of the Alabama National Guard, and veteran of the Gulf Wars, began organizing a plan of defense for Mobile. At his disposal he had about fifty older Blackhawk helicopters, a tank unit from Anniston, and about 4,000 National Guard and reservists, along with about 1,000 reserves, some from the state colleges and Universities. The

Mississippi, Northwest Florida and Georgia National Guards would also help. The National Guard and reserve units in Mobile had evidently put up a fight, but were not now communicating with his office in Montgomery. Early on March 12, two Blackhawks were dispatched to check out the situation.

WO3 Max Thackery and WO2 Joe Ballew were the pilots. Flying at a low altitude to avoid any radar detection, they flew from Montgomery, across the northwestern tip of Florida, down to I-10, and toward Mobile. Near the small town of Malibus, Max took his craft up for a look. What he spotted was a tanker in Mobile bay. That was all he ever told anyone! The explosion of a missile striking his Helicopter, stopped all communications! Joe reported, via a satellite, all that had happened. Gen. Hamilton sent three more copters with fully armed soldiers to get as close as they could to Mobile, and from there put a ground observation unit into place. He ordered all available tanks to go toward Mobile. They were loaded on trucks as fast as possible, but it would be at least twenty-four hours before they could have any effect on

the battle of Mobile.

From Satellite information, he could tell that there was a lot of activity, but the Chinese had started sending out a lot of misinformation, and were trying to jam all satellite and cell phone communications.

Ft. Rucker, Alabama, south of Montgomery, with its helicopter base had been wiped out. Fortunately, one group of four of the new Shadow helicopters had been on a training flight, and so, four of the newest helicopters were spared. They flew to the airport in Dothan. But, since they were on a training flight, they were not properly armed. Also Gunter Air Force Base on the north edge of Montgomery was nuked, but Montgomery itself received little damage.

About midday, Gen. Hamilton learned of the four Shadow helicopters that had escaped Ft. Rucker. These would have the latest in anti missile equipment and were almost undetectable by radar. In fact they were hard to see at all, and made very little noise. Sometimes they were spotted only by the shadow they cast on the ground, thus the name. He ordered these to Montgomery, to be fully armed. By 6:00 p.m. three helicopters were ready to go, with the fourth kept in reserve. He asked the chaplain to pray for them, and then he sent the three of them on a mission, from which he fully expected they would never return. **Attack the Tanker in**

Mobile Bay! WO1 Mel Hammond, WO2 Fran "the Fox" Schmidt, and WO1 Goal Washington were the pilots. WO1 Jo Ling, WO1 Suzy Mark, and WO1 Chuck Chissom were the copilots and missile guidance officers. All but WO2 Schmidt were fresh out of pilot training. Hugging the ground to avoid any possible radar detection, they spread out just east of Mobile Bay. When they went up to launch the attack, they were five miles apart. This would make it difficult for the Chinese to hit all three Shadows at once. True to their name, the Chinese did not detect the choppers until the first missiles struck home. The Chinese concentrated their missiles at the center Shadow, which was manned by WO2 Fran 'the Fox' Schmidt. 'The Fox' used his defensive maneuvers, sending out flares and chaff, then dove for the cover of the ground. The other two continued their attack and they were rewarded by a lot of secondary explosions. Evidently there were a large number of explosives still aboard the tanker. There was a huge column of smoke. Then the tanker tilted to one side and slid into Mobile Bay. Now it was up to the ground forces.

On the thirteen of March, Gen. Hamilton showed up with his tanks and the older Blackhawk helicopters. His first surprise was watching a Chinese transport circling to land at Mobile Regional Airport. The Blackhawks

were given the task of putting the transport out of business. As soon as the transport realized that it was under attack it tried to go out to sea and climb out of range of the helicopters. It was too late. The plane crashed on the beach at Gulf Shores (a favorite beach resort area). In the haste to down the transport, the Blackhawks were unaware of the missiles being launched at them from the airport. Three of the Blackhawks were knocked out of commission. One crashed near Tillmans Corner, one managed an emergency landing on Interstate 10 near Tillmans Corner, and the other went into the Bay. Only three soldiers survived.

It now seemed obvious that Mobile Regional Airport was in the hands of some foreign group. Gen. Hamilton ordered the helicopters to a small airfield near Fairhope, Alabama to refuel. Meanwhile, he and his staff tried to assess the situation. How many foreign troops were at the airport, how were they equipped, and were there other units in the Mobile area. For this project he called on the Shadow helicopters. Especially at night they could come and go without being detected. One hour after sundown the four Shadows went into the air with the best sensors the National Guard could put on them. If successful, they would be able to actually count the number of enemy soldiers at the airport, and detect any other significant movements by anyone. It was expected that there would be a minimum of civilian activity.

The report was surprising. There were at least 11,000 soldiers at the airport, and there was significant activity in the downtown area of Mobile. For the downtown area more information would be needed. It was decided to put a patrol on the ground as near downtown as possible. The 'Fox' flew 12 soldiers, led by Lt. James Boyd, in near the old Bay Bridge. From there they could infiltrate as close as possible into downtown, hoping to pick up information from any civilians who had not fled the area.

The patrol led by Lt. Boyd carefully worked their way along the abandoned streets, being careful to stay in the shadows. No street lights were working. They chose to go down through the CSX railroad yards. On they went to the State docks, where they worked their way through the many shipping containers, then up to Delchamps Drive, down to Water St. No activity was detected. Quietly they worked their way over to St. Anthony St. All of a sudden a shot was fired and Pfc. Sanders was on the ground. Then there were voices, and an avalanche of men shouting in a foreign tongue. Quickly they retreated back the way they had come dragging the wounded

Sanders with them. Finally they were back among the shipping containers. But the pursuit continued. The Lieutenant called for air support. Two Blackhawks were sent in. As soon as the Blackhawks began firing, the foreign troops withdrew. One Blackhawk settled to the top of a shipping container, and the twelve men climbed aboard and flew away. One thing was certain; something was going on in downtown Mobile.

General Hamilton now had a decision to make. Could he attack the force in Mobile without endangering the civilians? He decided that they would take back the airport first, then decide what had to be done with the downtown area.

At dawn on March 14, the troops, tanks and helicopters were in place for an all-out attack on the airport. First, the four chaplains who were accompanying the battle group prayed over the group. With the additions of Mississippi and Georgia troops, he now had about 8,000 soldiers. Also, from Birmingham Air Guard came five fully armed F-16s. With the Shadows' information gathered on the previous night, the F-16s led the battle. The suddenness of the attack caught the Chinese unprepared, but they did launch a number of antiaircraft missiles at the F-16s. The F-16s were equipped with some defensive weapons, such as flares and chaff. Only one F-16 was hit, and the pilot was able to eject. The Chinese were in disarray when the tanks and helicopters came charging in. Eventually they surrendered. The Americans lost one F-16, two tanks, one Blackhawk helicopter (plus the four lost before the big battle), and fifty-two men. The Chinese dead were 576, and around 10,000 captured.

After the fall of the airport, General Hamilton sent a unit into the downtown area bearing a white flag. The Chinese honored the gesture, by allowing the unit to come in unarmed. The offer was simple. Surrender and no one will be killed. The small force of Chinese in downtown quickly accepted the offer. As it turned out, there were only 250 foreign troops in the downtown area.

In the harbor the tanker was still visible, and the name could be read, Esfahan. It was the tanker that Joe and Rita Richardson had taken. When the Richardsons finally read about it, they knew that they had been witnesses to the start of the war. It had started several years before! Later they would find out that the Esfahan was being refitted in Shanghai for the mission to Mobile Bay. **That Day** was long in planning.

This was the second victory.

CHAPTER 8
ISRAEL MARCH 12

Israel was on high alert because of the worldwide situation. About 6:00 p.m. Israeli time a multiple missile launch was detected from Iran toward Israel. The Patriot-X s (an anti missile-missile) were activated and when the missiles from Iran were within range, the 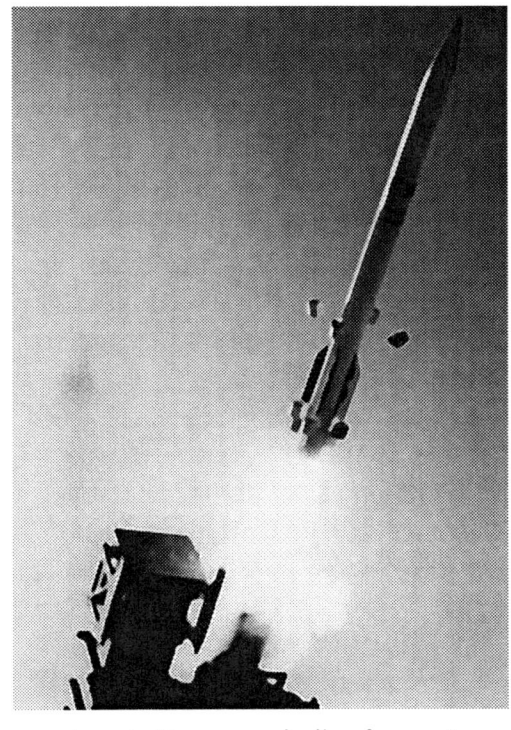 Patriot-Xs were launched. Every missile from Iran was killed. One missile detonated with a nuclear explosion over the western desert of Iraq.

By the morning of March 13, Israel was prepared with an immediate aerial attack against Iran. Before the attack, Captain Matthew Goldberg took off in a U-2, a high-flying observation aircraft. It took about an hour to reach a cruising altitude of 85,000 feet. At that altitude he could direct an attack from the airspace over Iraq and Kuwait and was out of range of most anti-aircraft missiles. Then Major Solomon Williams led the air attack of two flights of five fighter-bombers. They flew low to avoid radar detection over Jordan and across Saudi Arabia and Southeast across the United Arab Emirates, out across the Persian Gulf to the southwest border of Iran where they spread out. When they were within range, up they went up and launched the air to ground missiles immediately. Iran was ready, and launched a number of anti-aircraft missiles. The Israeli aircraft were prepared with a full spectrum of anti missile devices. Flares were dropped followed by hard banks to avoid heat-seeking missiles. Chad was spread to confuse the radar, followed by deep dives and the direction taken was back to Israel. Lasers were aimed at the anti-aircraft missiles from the U-2, to further confuse the guidance systems of the missiles.

Unfortunately, one aircraft was struck, and downed, followed by a parachute. Lt. Yishtak Zeewi successfully guided his parachute into the

Persian Gulf. An American helicopter rushed to the rescue. He was quickly snatched from the Gulf. Success.

Iran's nuclear program went up in a number of mushroom clouds, along with Tehran and Esfahan. It would be a long time before Iran was a nuclear threat again.

CHAPTER 9
THE ENEMY

By the 12th of March, President Jake Oderon had sufficient evidence that China, North Korea, Venezuela, Cuba and some Mideast group had organized the attack. Communications were complete with the allies of NATO and SEATO. Submarines from the fleet stationed at St. Mary's in Georgia were on their way for a counterattack. All available missiles were directed toward Chinese military and industrial sites. Although the United States was nearly destroyed, many nuclear and thermonuclear weapons were available. There was no response from Russia. Would Russia join the fight against America, simply sit on the sidelines waiting to take advantage of any situation which developed, or take a stand against the Chinese invasion? An additional question caused the President to prepare possible attacks against Russia. Did the Russians provide intelligence to China? But for the time being no action was being taken against Russia.

Was this a fatal mistake?

Immediate plans for an invasion of Cuba and China were made. Venezuela and the Middle East would be left for later. What military options were available? There were only about 1.5 million active duty personnel whose bases had been severely damaged, and about four million National Guard and Active Reserves, but many of these were stationed in the now destroyed cities. Against a standing armed force of more than fifty million, the odds were not good. Great Britain's one million could be counted on. Further, the NATO alliance could provide about three million more, but at least one million of these would be needed to provide defense for these countries. Australia had about five hundred thousand, and South Korea (along with the troops from the North) about one million. Canada would add another hundred thousand. Japan had about a five hundred thousand. Every other country had only enough to defend its own country.

All inactive personnel were directed to report to the nearest military base or armory and told to be prepared for duty. It would take time, but Chinese forces were even now invading many parts of the country. Would the simple mathematics of an overwhelming force just be too great?

CHAPTER 10
BATTLE OF WILMINGTON, DELAWARE

This is the story of Amoco Hooks. He was named Amoco because he was born at an Amoco Service Station. His mother Marshew was only fifteen at the time. He met his father, but never really grew up around him. His first home was in the housing projects with his grandmother, Malene Dillard. His mother finished high school and went to night school to earn a diploma in business administration. Then she was employed by an insurance agency.

One day Marshew came home from work and announced, "Old Man Dricker, the office manager, is retiring. They offered your Momma the job. We're going to move out of here and have our own house."

During the summer he turned eight, Amoco came to live in a house in South Philadelphia. Now Amoco had a new challenge. He was going to a new school. His first day, a boy named Morey asked him, "Are you going to gas up the school, Amoco?" drawing out the name for emphasis. All the boys laughed.

The next day Amoco was prepared. When Morey asked, "Hey Amoco, Are we gonna get a fillup today?" Amoco responded, "Hey Morey, if I smelled more like you maybe the girls would stay away from me, too, Morey." dragging out the Morey for emphasis. Everybody laughed, even Morey. After that he was just Amoco.

He was exposed to much of what was bad in South Philly. He managed to try drugs, but his mother found out. When he was sixteen, he got a girl pregnant. The mother opted for an abortion. Even while making good grades, he decided to drop out of school, but Marshew would have none of that.

Amoco loved butter. When Amoco was about eleven, he decided to butter his toast on both sides. When Momma came in and saw the mess she said, "Boy, don't you know that you can't butter both sides of the toast without making a mess." After that it became a saying around the house. Whenever Amoco made a mess of something, Momma would say, "Don't butter your toast on both sides. You can't be a part of a gang and be part of this family. It's just too messy."

Then when Amoco decided to drop out of school, Marshew reminded him that he couldn't run the streets, with, "You can't butter your toast on both sides. You can't get a good job without finishing high school. And you can't live here unless you are in school!" He graduated with honors while he was only seventeen.

After he turned eighteen in the summer, he joined the U.S. Army. He seemed to have a talent for mechanics. So the Army put him through Helicopter Mechanics School, at Ft. Rucker, Alabama. He spent one year in the Near East. He was promoted to E5 before his first three years were up. He elected not to reenlist. He quickly found out that jobs were not very abundant in Philly for a helicopter mechanic. Then he heard about an opening with the National Guard in New Castle, Delaware. This was just about an hour's drive from south Philly. He took the job as a civilian, but had to join the National Guard.

At 11:00 a.m. on March 11 (**That Day**), Amoco was at work. An armed helicopter had been brought in for repairs. His first order of business was to take the rockets and other munitions off and store them. Just then the nuclear bomb that destroyed Philadelphia shook the buildings and grounds, but did no substantial damage at the New Castle County Airport. Nobody seemed to know what had happened. What could have made such an impact? Then Amoco saw the mushroom cloud ascending above Philadelphia, and knew to take cover. Even if the explosion did not get them, then the radiation fallout might. Fortunately the National Guard had constructed an underground emergency shelter. That was where Amoco and the rest of the National Guard went for the remainder of the day and that night. Slowly the information trickled in. The United States had been attacked and most of the large cities were gone. By morning they knew that they would be called on for action somewhere.

When they emerged from the shelter on March 12, they encountered a huge surprise. Chinese soldiers were all over the place. What was going on? Major Yarnell, the commanding officer, went out to see what was happening. As soon as he stood up and waved his arm, he was shot. These people were not negotiating. Quickly everyone went back inside, and gathered all the arms they could find. Amoco went to a hanger where he had been working on a helicopter, to see if he could find some rockets or something. The Chinese attacked quickly. The twenty or so soldiers fought valiantly, but the fight was over in about ten minutes. Amoco watched in horror from the hanger. What few were not killed in the action, were finished off by the Chinese. No one else was left alive. Now Amoco had to find a place to hide until he could get out. He knew every inch of this hanger. He knew that there were crevasses along the rafters where a person could hide without being seen from the ground. He grabbed a water bottle and up he went. From there he watched as much as he could. The Chinese were setting up missiles, trying to get some of the helicopters running, and taking over the whole airport. He heard one of the helicopters take off and then land a few minutes later. They might be able to fly them, but to arm any of the missiles, they would have to know some of the codes. Then it occurred to him that the codes were locked in a vault. It would not take the Chinese long to open that antique. Since he was one of the few who knew the combination, he decided to wait for nightfall and go get the codes (if they were still there.)

At 8:00 p.m. he climbed down from his perch. He went under a loose panel at the back of the hanger, and went around to the back of the National Guard offices. Finding an unlocked window, he opened it with a little creak. No one noticed. Quickly he made his way down the familiar halls to the Major's office. Someone was in there. He needed a diversion. He went back to the hangar to see if he could launch a rocket, or some kind of weapon. He spotted a gas tank. He poured a trail from the loose panel to the underside of the helicopter, and sat the tank down there. It might set off the rockets still attached under the wing which had not been disarmed on the previous day. Back through the loose panel he went. Then he lit the gasoline trail and moved quickly back to the office building. Sure enough, the rockets exploded. The whole hanger seemed to hang in the air for a moment, then crashed down. The Chinese came from everywhere. Amoco made his way back to the now vacant office. He noticed several dents in the vault, obviously made by bullets. He opened the vault, retrieved the secret codes, closed the vault, and made his way back out the window. Now he needed a new hiding place. And he needed to burn the codes. Instead he found a ditch with water in it. He decided to tear the codes into small bits, soak them in water and scatter them far and wide. This he proceeded to do. Probably no one would notice the bits of paper scattered all over.

Now a hiding place was needed. He found one unguarded helicopter, and rolled into the back. He really needed sleep. The next morning it started raining like cats and dogs. He knew he had to get off the airport grounds. It was just a matter of time before they found him. The rain might be a good cover. So between the many hangars, and other buildings, he made his way out to the western side of the airport. Maybe some of the guards would be taking cover from the rain. He finally got near the fence that ran along the edge of the airport. But how was he going to get through the fence? Then he remembered that he had been carrying a pair of wire pliers with him for two days. He hadn't even noticed. Amoco slipped the pliers out, and with strong hands began clipping wires. About twenty minutes later he had a hole big enough to get through. But even through the fence, he knew that he was not safe and he was right next to

Airport Road. If he could just get across without being spotted, he might be able to find something to eat. Also, he wanted to report the status of his unit to someone higher. He found a few older houses on the other side of Airport Road. Now, if they don't shoot him on sight, maybe someone will let him eat and sleep. He banged on the door of the first house that was out of sight of the highway. He received a gruff reply from inside, "Go away. Haven't you already taken everything we have?" Grudgingly a middle-aged man's face appeared at the door.

Amoco quickly said, "Please let me in, but don't turn any lights on. I'm from the National Guard at the airport. They've killed everyone but me. Please, I'm very cold."

Slowly the man sized up the situation. "How did you escape? Come on in! We'll keep the lights off since we don't have any, since the bomb went off. The Chinese have come around and collected all our food, but we managed to hide a little."

Amoco related all that had happened, and requested a cell phone. Mr. Amos Peabody introduced himself and his wife, Joyce. "We might be able to keep you for one day, but by then we will be out of food. We do have plenty of water, but we don't know how contaminated it is. We are going to have to leave here ourselves, soon. But our cell phone is not working right now. I think that the towers are all down or without power. "

March 12: In New Jersey the remaining forces were quickly organized under the leadership of Lt. General Max Hardin. Ft. Dix had been surrounded by a battery of Patriot missiles and, so, was able to shoot down the two missiles which had been aimed at it. Also the base had a lot of extra soldiers on hand because of deployment orders. They were expected to be assigned to the Middle East. He had a few F-18s available, and about 50,000 healthy soldiers from Ft. Dix, National Guard from New York, Pennsylvania, Delaware, and New Jersey.

From ground information around Wilmington, Delaware, Gen. Hardin had learned that a sizable force had entered the city. In fact, the Chinese had overrun New Castle County Airport with the large National Guard presence. Two battalions of helicopters were stationed there along with a medical company. What little communications came out indicated that there was a very large group of Chinese troops at the airport. Not much else was known. But if it was like Mobile, Alabama, they probably came in by tanker, or possibly by plane. But other problems were facing the troops in New Jersey.

Before the group could launch an attack, they had to take cover. The radiation from the nuclear explosions over New York, Philadelphia, and Baltimore needed to blow out to sea. In particular, the nuclear cloud from Philadelphia was hanging over most of New Jersey. Therefore, the orders for March 12 were to take cover with no outside activities. All the National Guard and reserve units were ordered to stay away from Wilmington.

On the morning of March 13 the winds were more favorable. It appeared that the radiation was decreasing rapidly and rain had started. It came down in buckets. From 5:00 a.m. to 9:00 a.m. five inches of rain fell. This would help wash away some of the surface radiation. But extreme care was the order of the day. So much of the nation's military had been eliminated, it became more important to exercise caution. At the same time, foreign troops had been placed in Wilmington, Delaware. This situation was intolerable. It was the first time an enemy force from another continent had invaded the United States since the War of 1812. Gen. Hardin knew that something must be done soon. So, on the afternoon of March 13th he ordered surveillance aircraft to fly over Wilmington. Also, if the cloud cover could lift, satellite information could be used.

The first surveillance flight, an ancient RF-101 from the Air National Guard unit near Albany, New York, approached Wilmington. At 20 miles out of Wilmington, it was met with anti-aircraft missiles. The third missile struck home. Lt. Jeff George was able to eject, but had provided very little information. Next the Army launched ten drones. These unmanned aircraft, would provide valuable information if they could get close enough. By having all ten flying at close intervals of time from a variety of directions, maybe a couple would get through the defenses of the enemy. It worked. Actually three drones were able to send back a lot of information. One important piece of data was that the I-295 bridge over the Delaware River had been knocked out. The motivation for destroying the bridge was unclear. Another bit of information was that there was no tanker near Wilmington. There were a couple of cargo ships of the type that transport canisters. The antiaircraft fire had come from the ship in the Christina River nearest the Delaware River. Also, there were no large aircraft parked at New Castle County Airport. Gen. Hardin had enough information on troop location and the exact location of two Cargo ships in the mouth of the Christina River near the I-495 bridge. Also, this bridge appeared to be intact. Next he ordered two Pershing XI missiles to be fired against the cargo ship which was firing at our aircraft. Another RF-101 provided laser guidance from a distance of thirty miles (out of range of the anti-aircraft missiles), and was able to verify the hits. A lot of secondary explosions occurred. The ship tilted and slid into the Christina River.

At 3:15 p.m. Gen. Hardin received a surprise phone call. A Spec5 Amoco Hooks was on the line. Amoco talked fast, "They killed everyone but me. Major Yarnell tried to talk to them, but they shot him. Everyone else tried to shoot it out with them, but they were all killed. I hid in the hanger, and then remembered that the codes for arming the missiles on the helicopters were in the Major's office. So I managed to blow up the hanger as a diversion, and went to the Major's office and opened the safe, got the codes and destroyed them. They can't arm the missiles." General Hardin responded, "Well done, soldier. Talk to Captain Hodges and he'll tell you how to meet up with us."

Amoco had completed his mission when he found a working cell phone at a neighbor's house close to the Peabody's home. Furthermore, the General wanted his detailed information about the airport. Arrangements were made for Amoco to join up with the other troops out on Centre Road west of Wilmington on the morning of the fourteenth of March. A new hero was made!

With the cargo ship gone, the invaders only hope for reinforcements came from the New Castle County Airport. So the immediate need was to seal off the airport. Located in Annville, Pennsylvania, was a helicopter training base with several OH-58 Kiowa Helicopters. Gen. Hardin ordered them to pick up Army engineers from Middletown, Delaware, and take them close enough to the airport to allow them to infiltrate the enemy lines and blow up the runways.

During the past two days, John Montesi, a high school mathematics teacher in Middletown, Delaware, and his family had stayed in the basement of their house, hoping to minimize the effect of the radiation from the nuclear explosions in Baltimore and Philadelphia. Fortunately the winds had not carried the radiation toward Middletown. So he was not surprised when he received the phone call advising him to report to the National Guard Armory, but at 10:00 p.m.? He was part of the 249th Engineer Detachment of the Delaware National Guard. His speciality was the use of explosives. He had spent three years in the U.S. Army as an enlisted man with the engineers, then went to college. He majored in mathematics, with a minor in chemistry. He met Elizabeth (Dardin) in college. They were married upon her graduation at the end of his sophomore year. She taught school while he finished his degree. Upon graduation he applied to become an officer with the Delaware National Guard. With depleted numbers since the Gulf Wars, he was accepted almost immediately. He completed Officer Candidate School in the summer after his graduation, and began teaching that very fall. Mathematics teachers were in short supply, so he was hired on the condition of completing some education courses. Now he was a weekend warrior, teacher, husband, soon to be a father, and part time student. That fall Elizabeth became pregnant. His only daughter, Sara, was now two years old. He had been promoted to 1st Lieutenant on his daughter's first birthday. With the extra income from the National Guard, Elizabeth had become a full time mom. She did some tutoring on the side, but her delight was dark headed, blue-eyed Sara.

At the armory Lt. Montesi met with his crew for the job ahead. The orders were curt: "Blow up the runways at New Castle County Airport. The airport is in the hands of the enemy, and we suspect that reinforcements will be flown in at any moment." With the orders was a detailed layout of the airport. Quickly the crew of three men and one woman assembled the necessary explosives and detonators for the job. While they waited at the helicopter pad, the Lt. went over the details of the job. It would be necessary to split into two pairs and place the explosives at the intersections of the longest runways. This would disable the runways, so that no large aircraft could land. Before he was finished, the helicopters landed. Once aboard, Lt. Montesi finished going over the plans, and the urgency of the mission. Because of the size of the load they were to carry, they were only armed with pistols. However, under no circumstances were they to initiate contact with the enemy.

The helicopters could not get close to the airport accept by flying low over the Delaware

River. The four engineers hopped out of the helicopters on the bank of the river at Army Creek. It was about two miles to the airport and another mile inside the airport grounds to the two best sites. There were no cars on the roads, so they had to conceal themselves between the buildings and landscape. By 4:00 a.m., March 14, the engineers, Lt. John Montesi, S.Sgt. Vance Wiley, Pfc. Tamara Ramage, and Pfc. Ralph Frank, had the explosives in place. Slowly they retreated from the airport property. By daybreak they were far enough away to detonate the explosives. When the Chinese heard the explosions, they scrambled all over the airport property trying to locate the infiltrators. It would be a while before any large aircraft could land on the runways at New Castle

County Airport. By then the engineers were off the property, and successfully concealing themselves among the warehouses along Churchmans Road. Here they used cell phones to send out the message, "Runways crippled at the appropriate points." They hid until nightfall and then made their way back to the rendezvous spot by the river. By the time they arrived at the pickup point, the battle over the airport was in full swing. The helicopters never arrived.

Now the real attack on the foreigners could take place. With helicopters and trucks, Gen. Hardin got the troops, tanks, and aircraft into position to launch the attack late in the day of March 14. At 6:00 p.m. he sent a Hummer in with a white flag. At first the invaders shot at the vehicle, but quickly stopped. The Hummer was allowed in. Lt. Forrest Macon carried the terms of surrender to the Chinese. The Chinese were incensed over the offer. The reply was curt, "We have destroyed the United States of

America. You have no army or air force. We only wish to occupy Wilmington peacefully. Do not attempt to stop us or you will be annihilated."

By 8:00 p.m. all forces were in place. Attack aircraft went first. Two old B-52s rained bombs

down from a very high altitude. Then five Air National Guard F-16 fighter-bombers were sent in, followed by the MI-24 Hind attack helicopters. Next came the artillery. The battle was intense.

Missiles were flying everywhere from both sides. At 10:00 p.m. the tanks were sent in, followed by foot soldiers, some with shoulder fired missiles. By the time the tanks reached the middle of the airport, the Chinese were flying their own white flags. The battle stopped just as suddenly. Three of the five F-16s were downed. Four MI-24 Hind helicopters were hit. Two tanks were blown up. All together the Americans lost six airmen, 165 soldiers in helicopters, tanks and on the ground plus another 224 wounded. There were eleven hundred dead Chinese on the airport grounds plus those killed on the tanker. The remaining 3,500 Chinese surrendered. The Battle of Wilmington was over.

At 2:00 a.m. on the 15th, Lt. Montesi decided to turn his cell phone back on. He was greeted with a message almost immediately. "Return to the airport. It is in the hands of our brave soldiers." Now the crew questioned the necessity of their mission. But later it was determined that two large aircraft had approached the airport during the morning of March 14. If these aircraft had supplied reinforcements for the Chinese, then the outcome of the battle may have been very different.

With the radiation decreasing rapidly, the

next order of business for the soldiers was to maintain order, and begin supplying the Northeast with needed food and water supplies, along with medical help.

CHAPTER 11

BATTLE OF FT. LAUDERDALE, FLORIDA

At about the same time a new threat came from Cuba. The long suppressed Cuba now had a powerful friend, and trained soldiers. Cuban soldiers came ashore at Ft. Lauderdale in landing craft from a cruise ship. They quickly seized the airport (mostly undamaged from the bombs which struck Miami and Homestead). The National Guard of Southern Florida was simply out manned and out gunned. The Airbase at Homestead had been dealt a lethal blow from short range missiles based in Cuba, so no help could come from the local Air Force. The Guard retreated toward Ft. Myers, in hopes of gathering strength from other National Guard units, and possibly some regulars from other branches of the service.

March 11: On the West Coast, an UPS flight from China had been diverted from destroyed San Francisco to Sacramento. A FedEx flight was also diverted to Sacramento. They arrived within minutes of one another. Both planes pulled to a stop near the control tower. The cargos were not Chinese-made goods, but the Chinese themselves. They quickly forced their way into the control tower and began taking over the airport. National guard and regular units from all over California were called to stop this. But within the hour, several more planes from China were landing, and within a few hours, the troop strength was at about 10,000. This was a major invasion point. In the two days before the U.S. Army and Air Force could find sufficient units to stop the inbound flights, there were about 200,000 fully armed Chinese in place around Sacramento.

Where had these Chinese invaders come from? What did they hope to attain? Did they truly wish to own America?

As soon as the National Guard in Florida heard about the takeover in Sacramento, They immediately started for Ft. Lauderdale, with a lot of shoulder launched missiles. The idea was to stop foreign troops from using the airport as a landing spot. But the Cubans had taken up positions all around the airport and outward for ten miles. It would be hard to infiltrate their lines. Major Charles Harris devised a plan. Launch an attack on the western perimeter with artillery, missiles and any air support which could be brought into play. This would engage most of the Cubans. While the fight was going on, infiltrate a few squads of infantry with missiles to the ocean side, east of the airport, from where any foreign planes would probably choose to land.

And so Captain Lewis and Lt. Jarvis headed up the infiltration squads. Captain Lewis explained the objective, "We're going across Lake Okeechobee and into the Everglades, through the West Palm Beach Canal. Make our way through the darkened streets of Coral Springs and down to Pompano Beach. Then we are going to post ourselves in the parking decks nearest the airport, and wait for any enemy planes to fly in. Questions?" Pfc. Groggan responded, "How are we going to get back out?" Cpt. Lewis answered, "We expect that there will be a minimum of soldiers guarding that end of the field, and we will fight our way out if necessary." They proceeded as planned. Then along the Inland Waterway, on southward past the stranded cruise ship, *The Rotterdam*. Very carefully they passed several guards and located themselves in a parking deck. At about daybreak on the 13th of March, the attack on the western perimeter began.

Almost immediately a Chinese cargo plane started its descent to the airport, being careful to avoid the conflict in the west. When the plane got within range, the American missiles were launched. In order to bypass any anti missile devices on board the Chinese plane, the missiles went out at five second intervals. It worked! The third wave found the mark, and the plane went down in flames. But that brought a lot of notice from the local guards. A full firefight broke out. But the Cubans were seriously undermanned on this side of the airport. The Americans' position in the parking deck along with some good observation of the Cubans' positions worked wonders. The Cubans were quickly overpowered and the few men left standing retreated toward the airport. But a counterattack was sure to come. The Americans disappeared back into the swamp.

But the attack on the Chinese plane, brought an unexpected surprise for the troops under Major Harris who was on the western side of the airport. The Cubans saw and heard the crash and, evidently, suspected that a major attack was coming from the ocean side. Quickly they diverted most of their forces to the other end of the airport. When the Cuban force started moving troops away from the west, Major Harris thought that they were in full retreat. So he gathered everything they had and launched an attack.

Before they knew it, they were on the airport property.

Then suddenly the U.S. Navy brought in air support out of Puerto Rico. Making radio contact with Major Harris' unit, they came in hard and with scorching results totally defeated the Cubans. Some stragglers were rounded up, and the airport was secure for now.

CHAPTER 12
CORPUS CHRISTIE, TEXAS

Lance Lopez was born in Norias, Texas, only about 25 miles from the Gulf of Mexico. He was the oldest of five children, two brothers and two sisters. His father, Guadalupe Lopez (named for the city from which his father immigrated to the U.S.) worked on one of the oil rigs in the Gulf of Mexico. They were middle class economically, but Guadalupe was away more than he was at home.

On Lance's sixth birthday he finally saw the Gulf of Mexico. He couldn't believe how big it was. Instantly he fell in love with the sea, and would sneak off at times, to once again gaze at the vastness of that great water. Lance was an athlete in school, playing soccer, basketball, and baseball. He was a good athlete, but not good enough to garner a scholarship to any college. Two weeks after graduating, Lance came to his mother and said, "Mom, you know that I have always loved the sea. So now, I'm going to enlist in the Navy."

THAT DAY

After completing basic training at Great Lakes, he applied for the Navy Seals, a specialized unit which underwent intensive training. He first went to Coronado, California, for six months of intensive training, with three weeks at Ft. Benning, Georgia, for paratrooper training. They were the undersea divers, demolition teams, first units at the front of any battle, and highly respected throughout the U.S. Navy.

Afterwards, he was stationed at Newport News, Va., for another eighteen months of additional training. Then he went to the Persian Gulf for action early in the Iraq invasion.

From the U.S. Navy: *A Navy Sea, Air and Land, or SEAL, special operations officer, noted that some of his unit's missions throughout Iraq from April to October included protecting a key dam, finding and capturing remnant regime members and foreign terrorists, seizing enemy ordnance.* Lance was part of this.

While stationed in Virginia, Lance met Nandy. He saw her first on a street with friends. Her eyes flirted with his for a brief moment. Lance made it his business to find out more about this young lady. After duty one Friday, Lance saw her again near the post pharmacy. He eased over to her and said, "Hi." She responded with, "Hi, yourself." He was surprised with this and answered, "Say, my name is Lance. Me and my friends are going to get an ice cream. Want to come along?" Her reply was short, "You expect to pick me up on a street corner?" Lance said with a little pout, "Well, I can't pick you up at your house. I don't know where you live." She laughed and stated,"My name is Nandy. And you'll just have to find out where I live. Treat me to an ice cream without your friends and we'll see." Lance said, "Well, come on.", and turned to his friends and said, "See you guys." Lance found out that she was a Captain's daughter and lived off base. He invited her to movie on Saturday night. She accepted, but said that she would meet him at the theater. It became a regular sequence of events.

When her parents found out whom she was seeing, they were adamantly opposed. Then with his trips overseas and time on board ship, there was a continuing battle. Finally Nandy ended the love/hate situation by announcing that she had found someone else. The other guy did not exist, but Lance would not find out about that until much later.

He was promoted to E4 by the end of his first enlistment, and offered a substantial amount of money to reenlist. Lance was promoted twice over the next two years, but was busted after a rather vicious fight in a bar near the base in Virginia. He took the next thirty days on leave and went home. It was March 2, 20XX, just nine days before **That Day**. It was a few days of relaxing while Lance was considering what his next options were. Should he leave the Navy at the first opportunity, or stick around and see if the promotions came fast? He knew that he had many friends in the SEALs. Some would probably want him to continue his outstanding work. A few would think that he had betrayed them all.

All that changed on March 11. By noon, Lance was hearing all the news about attacks on America. He couldn't believe what he was hearing. How could the most powerful nation on earth not have a way of preventing such an attack? What were the people at Homeland Security doing? Also what could Lance do now?

Around 3:00 p.m., March 11: In Corpus Christi, a tanker had started launching boats, and firing missiles. The first volley was two nuclear weapons aimed at Kingsville Naval Air Station. One was a dead hit, and the other landed on King's Ranch. Lance could see the nuclear mushroom cloud from his home. He then knew that he must do all in his power to help out, but it was unclear, at first, where or when.

Later Lance would learn that the Corpus Christi Naval Air Station was attacked with a massive number of conventional weapons. There was neither helicopter nor plane left undamaged. The Chinese intelligence was very good. So. . . . no Naval Air Support could be counted on. Also, San Antonio and the bases around it were wiped out. The Chinese troops flooded in, with little opposition. Their first target was the Naval Air Station. The Navy gave a valiant fight, but in the end they had little left to fight with, after the initial missile attack. The Chinese just flooded in. Every sailor on the base was killed in the fight, or simply lined up and shot. They were taking no prisoners. The only thing left undamaged at the Naval Air Station were the runways.

Next they took over the television station and began putting out their propaganda. They overran the police and sheriff's offices. Anyone giving any opposition was simply shot. The city and the airfield were in enemy hands. Then they attacked the Corpus Christie International Airport. The opposition was minimal. The news from Corpus Christie was extremely bad.

National Guard and Reserves from Brownsville and up to Laredo began to form a sizeable group. From Victoria and surrounding areas the troops answered the call. Retired Gen. Andrew Summers (who lived on a ranch near Cuero, about 75 miles from San Antonio) took over command of the group. He was a battle-hardened soldier from the Gulf Wars.

The nearest National Guard unit to Norias (Lance's home) was in Weslaco, near Brownsville. That's where Lance headed. He found out that they were heading to Beeville, Texas, about forty miles north of Corpus Christie. There they met with General Summers, and Lance was elated to find two other seals, Petty Officer 2nd Class Jeff

Baumer, Petty Officer 3rd Class James Gurley. Lance had served with these two, so he knew how well they could perform.

March 12: The first order of business for the General was to destroy the tanker. Where could he get some air support? None was immediately available. How about some shoulder launched missiles? The Guard had quite a few of these. It would take several hits to destroy the tanker. Among his command he found the three Navy Seals. They would have to do the job. He consulted with the three. In spite of his recent reduction in rank, Lance was put in charge of the group Lance told the General, "Sir, if a diversion can be created, then we can get close enough to launch a lot of shoulder fired missiles. We can drag them along under water from the opposite side of the bay and get close enough to make sure we hit the ship. Or we could just place some explosives under the ship, itself." Gen. Summers took about an hour discussing the options with his staff, and called Lance back. "We have a lot of armor piercing shoulder launched missiles, so let's do it that way." Lance replied, "Aye, aye, sir."

The plan: Send out an attack, by whatever boat could be found, toward the NAS (where the Chinese had massed). Whoever took this mission had little chance of survival. Twenty volunteers came forward.

Another bad bit of news came from some observers from Corpus Christie. Three large aircraft had landed at the airport. There may be more. Also, the Chinese were sending out unmanned drones to observe the surrounding area. The Guard did have a mobile radar unit, and this was set up, so the drone was detected, and shot down, but the Chinese fired a couple of missiles at the radar station. One hit the antennae. The radar was out of business. General Summers gave the order to disperse and conceal all weapons.

March 13: Local clergymen and women offered prayers for protection and a successful mission. The volunteers commandeered ten boats, and came up from Padre Island. About midnight they came under the bridge with guns and shoulder launched missiles firing. The Chinese concentrated a very strong salvo at the ten boats. The battle was over in just fifteen minutes. All ten boats were sunk. Later, a lone survivor, Sgt. Louis Harris, managed to swim ashore and work his way along the bay until he was clear of the Chinese.

Meanwhile, the three Navy Seals were dragging their deadly load underwater to the northern shore of Corpus Christi Bay past the exhibit of the U.S.S. Lexington, down to the Marina, where they found plenty of cover. While the battle was engaged in full force on the other side, the three began the most crucial mission that Texas had seen since the Mexican War. From under the docks, they launched eighteen missiles in just five minutes. The tanker began exploding from inside. Now it would be up to our ground forces to stop the remaining Chinese. It would take time to get enough forces in place. But at least the Chinese had no supply ship to help them. Most of the heroes of this battle lay dead in the bay. They had helped save Texas from an invasion. One day their names would be placed on a plaque by the bay. The three Navy Seals managed to slip back into the water and escaped detection by the Chinese. Twenty-three men and women of our armed forces managed to kill more than 1,000 Chinese and destroy their supplies. It was a fine victory in an otherwise dismal war.

But the Chinese were still in possession of the Airport and Naval Air Station. The next order of business was to make sure that no other airplanes landed. At Texas A & M University, Corpus Christie, was a large contingent of ROTC. Some had been trained to handle anti-aircraft missiles. So far the Chinese had ignored the University. General Summers asked a group of soldiers to smuggle some missiles onto campus. A Lt. Rogers had graduated just last summer. With his knowledge of the campus, he was put in charge of the unit.

General Summers called him in, "Lt. Rogers, I understand that you recently graduated from Texas A&M here in Corpus Christie." Lt. Rogers, "Yes sir." Gen. Summers continued, "We need to stop any more aircraft from landing at the Naval Air Station, and the main airport. Can you smuggle a few ground to air missiles onto the campus, and get them close enough to shoot down anything trying to land?" Rogers, "Sir, I will need about ten men who are trained on the missiles, and we can do it. I worked in maintenance on the campus, and I believe that we can get a good observation spot, and a hiding place, if needed." Gen. Summers, "See Major Diego, and he will find the right men for you. As soon as you get the equipment and men, get down to the campus. We can't afford for the Chinese to receive more reinforcements. And thank you. God speed."

They had no problem smuggling the missiles onto campus. Then they recruited several ROTC men and women. They briefed them on the mission ahead, and the dangers. Lt. Rogers stayed with his new command and sent the rest of the regulars back to Gen. Summers with a large group of ROTC volunteers. Getting into position to shoot down any plane trying to land would be easy. The difficult part would be to escape after doing so. As part of his job, he advised the faculty and students who remained, to abandon the college. If they shot down any aircraft, the Chinese would be all over them. He didn't share this part of the plan with the faculty.

General Summers and his staff concentrated on finding some air support. Finally the news came that one B2 (B2 bombers were almost invisible to radar, but flew at subsonic speeds.) which had escaped being hit was at the Springfield, Missouri, airport. It was fully loaded. General Summers received word that it could bomb the two airfields, but needed additional data on the exact locations of the enemy weapons. The next satellite would not fly over the

area until 4:15 p.m., March 14. Whatever information it could send back would have to do.

That night the B2 made a bombing run at 1:00 a.m., March 15. The glow from the attack could be seen from a great distance. The B2 bombed the Naval Air Station and the cargo planes at the International Airport. A second blow against the Chinese had been taken. General Summers and his staff now believed that the Chinese could receive no more fresh supplies. But the longer the enemy held out the greater the risk of renewed weaponry. An attack against the NAS was necessary.

A land attack was complicated by the

location of the Naval Air Station and the location of Corpus Christie itself. Corpus Christie is surrounded by water to the Northeast and southeast and by land that is not easily negotiated to the southwest. I-37 courses down between Nueces Bay and the International Airport. To the west there is Texas 44 which goes right by the International Airport and County Highway 565 (Old Brownsville Road) which goes between the International Airport and a smaller Cuddihy Airport (not occupied by the Chinese).

The International Airport would have to be dealt with first. It was believed that this airport was not occupied by either a large or well armed force. It was decided to hit this airport with a quick strike force of well trained soldiers and marines by daybreak on the 15th. It was hoped that the Chinese would be a bit disorganized by the preceding air strike. There were a few helicopters and several tanks were available. The tanks were equipped with anti missile weapons. Then while this battle was attracting the Chinese's attention the main group would be working there way through the more difficult route around to the southwest, where, it was hoped, that the Chinese had not placed a large defensive group.

If the airport could be secured quickly, then most of this force could start toward the Naval Air Station. If they met substantial opposition, they were to fall back to the airport and take up defensive positions. If no large force met them, then they would divide into two groups and secure the bridges to the Naval Air Station. The attack on the International Airport went well. Our intelligence was good. Now Colonel Harvey was placed in charge of securing the Airport along with the prisoners.

Only three bridges connect Corpus Christie with the peninsula on which the NAS is located. The 358 bypass would be heavily guarded. Spur 3 through the Texas A & M campus would also draw a lot of attention, and it was highly exposed. The General had to be ready to follow up with a large attack. It was a classical military plan. Send the smaller but noisy force down I-37 and around the Texas 358 bypass. The main force would need to get south of Tailings Pond and some tanks might get across Yorktown Bridge. This would be difficult. The terrain was not inviting. So the three prong attacks were implemented on the morning of March 15. Since the Chinese had bigger plans for occupation of Texas, they had not blown up any of the bridges.

The group heading down 358 encountered a flag waving group of citizens. They immediately advised everyone to seek shelter. A battle was imminent, and sure enough the group was attacked before getting close to the bridge, and fell back, hoping to draw off a large group of Chinese. The second group launched their attack across the Yorktown Bridge, and actually managed to get across the bridge, before encountering a large group of heavily armed Chinese. They had to retreat back across the bridge, and to stop the Chinese counter attack, they blew up the bridge. The main body was late in showing up. The route they took was more treacherous than they imagined, so they didn't get by Tailings Pond until 3:00 p.m. But the attack on the Chinese near the Yorktown Bridge did catch the Chinese by surprise. The Chinese unit was wiped out. Next they managed to take the south side of the 358 bridge and thus split the Chinese forces. Several skirmishes took place over the next twenty-four hours. Both sides were holding their own.

By the morning of the March 17 they launched their attack on the airfield. At the first light of morning they saw a large plane circling to land but were not in position to shoot it down. All of a sudden several streaks of fire went up from Texas A&M campus and the plane went down in flames. Lt. Rogers and his group had come through. Then the real attack began. One group stayed at the bridge to prevent the Chinese from getting any reinforcements, and the rest attacked the now undersized group at the NAS. The Chinese were well armed and in good position for defense of the airfield. Missiles were flying everywhere. General Summers actually did not enter the airfield grounds until the 17th. The casualties were very high on both sides. By 9:00

a.m. the Chinese finally surrendered. American dead were more than twenty-three hundred. Chinese dead were about five thousand.

Still, the battle was not over. There was a substantial group of Chinese in and around Corpus Christie. General Summers sent a Hummer across the bridge with a white flag flying. It was an offer to the remaining Chinese to surrender. Since the ranking officers had been captured at the NAS, the remaining Chinese were very confused about what to do. General Summers gave them until 5:00 p.m. to surrender or die. At 4:30 the Chinese responded. A GMC Suburban came across the bridge with a white flag. They had chosen to surrender.

The battle of Corpus Christie was over, but with heavy casualties.

Lance Lopez received a battlefield commission for his participation in the conflict. As soon as he could, he asked to be released to go back to Virginia. He drove his old Chevrolet up through central Texas, avoiding the bombed out cities of Houston and Dallas, but through Little Rock, Arkansas where he spent the night. The next day he drove through Memphis, Nashville and Knoxville, Tennessee, where he was forced to spend the night because of curfews. The third day he drove through Bristol on the Tennessee-Virginia border. In Bristol gasoline was hard to find, but his uniform helped. Then he went up through Roanoke and down through Richmond and on to Petersburg. From there he headed to Suffolk where Nandy lived.

There he searched for and found Nandy and her mother. When Nandy saw him, she was all over him. She blurted, "Daddy was on the base when the bomb went off. Everybody was killed. I'm so glad to see you." Even Nandy's mom, Mrs. Kendricks, gave him a hug. Lance started explaining about the battle in Corpus Christie, but Nandy interrupted, "You've got bars!" (Referring to the Lt. bars on his shoulders.)

Lance explained, "Two other Seals and I sunk the big tanker in Corpus Christie Bay. General Summers thought it was a big deal and commissioned me. Is there anywhere we can go for a little while?"

Mrs. Kendricks joined in, "I'm going to see if I can round up some food. You two can stay here until I get back. It may take a while, since there are lines everywhere."

When she came back Nandy spoke first. "Mom, Lance and I are going to get married. Now please don't argue." Mrs. Kendricks, "I think that's wonderful. When?"

Lance, "As soon as we can clear the legal hurdles, Mrs. Kendricks."

Mrs. Kendricks, "Well, Lance, why don't you call me Laura or Mom, then. I believe that we are going to be family."

Lance, "OK, Laura. Now I would like to tell you both about the fight where I got busted. One guy was referring to Captain Kendricks in some very derogatory terms. I tried to get him to shut up, and he started swinging. I only defended myself, but all of his buddies lined up behind him and said that I started it. I'm really sorry. I should never have been in that place to begin with."

Laura, "You didn't need to explain, but thank you anyway. You two have my blessings. The Navy has set up a temporary headquarters right here in town for all the personnel who were off base on That Day. I'm sure you can find some help down there."

Two days later, Lance and Nandy were married at the local Methodist Church. After a few days Lance knew that he was needed somewhere. After making some inquiries, he found out that the nearest Navy base still in full operation was St. Mary's submarine base in Georgia. On March 22 he was assigned to a sub. The sub was headed to the Western Pacific.

CHAPTER 13

THE EMERGENCY PLAN

President Oderon and his cabinet had many more problems. A counter attack must be launched, the population must have safe water and be fed and housed. The wounded had to be looked after. The thousands dying from radiation needed care.

Congress met quickly on the 12th of March, and gave the President full power to order martial law, and declared war on: China, Cuba, and Venezuela. Whatever actions were necessary, President Oderon now had the authority to make. But did he actually have enough military and civilian manpower to carry out the necessary actions? Where would the equipment, food, water, clothing, transportation and other necessities come from? Communications had to be established with all concerned. Cabinet members and lower echelon personnel needed direction.

Priority one: Stop the invasion. To do this, a plan was formulated to defend our borders, airfields, ports and nationalize the National Guard. Call in all reserve military personnel, regardless of age. Launch immediate attacks on points of entry by foreign troops. The President and staff needed more information. By March 13, it became apparent that the Chinese were sending as many troops to invade America as could possibly be transported (and in whatever fashion) to our land. So far, submarines had placed people in our ports, domestic aircraft had delivered soldiers to any airfield possible, and tankers had been used to supply both troops, equipment and munitions. Our cities and military had been destroyed. Obviously other attempts would be made to carry out even more devastating attacks.

To this end, the leaders welcomed the news of the victories at Mobile, Ft. Lauderdale and Corpus Christie. At the same time, the United States was in dire straits. This was an epoch battle of the wounded tiger. The President and his staff knew that, somehow, they must survive.

Priority two: An immediate attack on China. Where were the vulnerable points in China? Intelligence was desperately needed. Some Chinese missiles did not hit the intended target. A missile with a nuclear warhead exploded south of the Tennessee River in North Alabama, leaving Redstone Arsenal and Marshall Spaceflight Center unharmed. From Redstone Arsenal a series of satellites was ordered launched.

Surprisingly, almost everything needed for satellite surveillance was in place. Hunt down and destroy all Chinese naval vessels. Request (or demand) help from NATO, SEATO and Russia and possibly Israel.

Priority three: To provide for the American people, Director of Homeland Security John Taylor was put in charge with full authority over everything but the military which was needed in the other priorities. This may be the largest problem. No one knew how bad the problem really was. Surely hungry people would resort to riots and looting. It was known that most American families only had enough food and water for a few days. The National Guard would have an additional task: Secure all food and water, so that an orderly distribution might take place. If this was not in place by the 16th of March, all bets were off as to how well behaved the citizens would be in this crisis.

CHAPTER 14
LOUISVILLE, KENTUCKY

Cory B. O'Reiley was born on a farm in western Kentucky, far from any city. When he was just 10 years old, his father took a job in Louisville as a fireman. His father, Lon O'Reiley had finally given up on keeping the family farm. After years of trying to compete with the big companies and seeing his family exist on next to nothing, he sold the farm, and paid off all the loans. Next he went to the big city of Louisville. There he had landed a position with the fire department as a fireman. It certainly was not a *get rich quickly scheme*, but he could put groceries on the table. There was enough left from the sale of the farm to make a substantial down payment on a house. Cory and his three sisters (one older, the other two younger) were not very happy with the change. Cory really missed the fields and the creek that ran along the edge of the farm, but in time he adjusted. He was enrolled in public school, and did O.K. His only extracurricular activity was track. He loved to run. He soon found out that no one could outrun him in the 5km races. He won the 5k in every city meet as a senior. He took second place in the state meet that year. He even threw the shot put and discus for best distances at his high school, but did not finish high enough at the state meet to earn any metals.

After graduation, he worked in a couple of different fast food restaurants. He really didn't like this kind of work. His family encouraged him to go to college, but there was very little money. Just after Christmas, he joined the U.S. Army. He was strong and worked hard. After basic training he was sent to Redstone Arsenal in North Alabama for maintenance training on some shoulder launched missiles systems. These were the type of missiles which were used to shoot down low flying aircraft. He loved this job. During his first three year hitch he served one year in Afghanistan, and was promoted to Spec5(E5).

After getting his discharge, he headed back to Louisville, and enrolled in the University of Louisville. Knowing he needed some extra money, he joined the National Guard and became a weekend warrior. Then he met Hannah. They were married and she kept working while Cory was going to school. At the National Guard he was promoted to Staff Sergeant (E6) that very year.

Louisville had been spared the nuclear destruction suffered by other river cities. On March 11, all available security forces, including police, state enforcement agencies, National Guard, and sheriffs were put on full alert by Governor Kile Willis. At about three p.m., March 11, some UPS planes began arriving from the Far East. Fortunately Louisville International Airport was still open. The first two did not stop at the usual terminal, but stopped near the control tower. The controllers in the tower ordered the planes to turn back because of other aircraft trying to land. (All commercial aircraft had been ordered to land, and because many airports were no longer capable of handling any incoming flights, Louisville was a natural place to divert a huge number of flights.)

Once stopped, the same pattern of occupying the control tower which was seen in Sacramento, was about to take place. Fully armed soldiers quickly surrounded the control tower. Explosives placed against the entry were very effective. The soldiers quickly took over the control tower. Almost all control tower personnel were killed on the spot. This caused some problems for planes trying to land. Most were diverted to some other field. One 747 crashed into a Skybus on the ground. There were no survivors on either plane.

Unfortunately, the crash did not block the longest runway, because more UPS planes were coming in. Next they attacked the lightly guarded Standiford Field Air National Guard. The few Airmen guarding the C-130s and C-5s were quickly overwhelmed. All were methodically killed. Several planes disgorged thousands of Chinese troops. The airport was simply in the hands of the Chinese. Within two hours there were about seven thousand Chinese on the grounds and they were fully armed. One C-5 did take off. Was it manned by Americans?

Upon hearing this bit of news, Governor Willis (a former major in the National Guard) ordered the National Guard to engage the enemy with all due haste. The Chinese must be stopped. All flights from foreign countries were ordered to be shot down. Only the Governor could give permission to land. This was also communicated to the Pentagon. S.Sgt. O'Reiley was ordered to the Armory on Crittenden Drive. He was in charge of all small missile systems.

March 12: It was late morning before S.Sgt. O'Reiley and the Guard could place some shoulder-launched missiles near the airport. He left two soldiers in a ditch near the airport with instructions to shoot down any aircraft trying to land. (By now all aircraft in the United States had been ordered to land and not to take off until further orders.)

The Chinese quickly expanded their control out onto I-65. They commandeered many cars, trucks, and buses. Into downtown Louisville they poured. The National Guard Armory next to the fairgrounds on Crittenden Dr. was targeted. A brief firefight took place. One Abram's Tank was armed and ready to go when the attack came. It did do some damage, but was knocked out by a shoulder-launched missile. The small Guard unit killed more than two hundred Chinese, but the Chinese kept coming. It appeared that the Chinese were willing to sacrifice any number just to win some strategic location. The Chinese won the battle, mainly on superior numbers. When Maj. Corvan realized that they were going to be overrun, he ordered Sgt. O'Reiley to escape, so that he could report the situation to others.

Sgt. O'Reiley commandeered the first vehicle that came his way. He headed downtown to the City Hall. The guards at City Hall were a little unwilling to allow a fully armed soldier to come in. So S.Sgt. O'Reiley had to remove all his weapons, and armored vest to gain entry. By the time he did this the Mayor (Hon. Ralph Williams) had come down to see what the ruckus was all about. S.Sgt. O'Reiley gave him a complete rundown. All police and Sheriff's deputies were ordered to enforce martial law upon the city. Citizens were warned to stay off the streets.

Cory O'Reiley called his wife, and then his parents with the severe warnings. Units of the National Guard from outside Louisville were assigned to bring order, and to make sure that food, water and other supplies were protected and made available to the population. Some rioting had already begun. Several super markets had already been vandalized. The Governor gave the order to shoot any looters. Bringing about order was a necessity. All National Guard personnel were ordered to Louisville.

Other bad news was that Ft. Campbell in southern Kentucky had been wiped out by an atomic bomb. All the soldiers who had been off base or who had somehow managed to survive were ordered to join up with the National Guard.

The Chinese attacked or knocked out all radio, television and cell phone towers except local channel 11, which was targeted for a takeover. After a very brief battle with security personnel, the station and the broadcasting tower were in the hands of the Chinese. Immediately the Chinese began broadcasting programs containing messages from Premier *On*. The messages were quite simple. "The Chinese Army is now in charge of the country, and there is no need for any more people to be injured. Further resistance is futile. In the end the United States will be a Chinese territory. Etc., etc."

March 13: By noon the Kentucky National Guard and other military personnel were near the south end of Louisville International Airport. They had attack helicopters and shoulder launched missiles, which could bring down any aircraft trying to land. Therefore, the Chinese were limited to what they already had, and anything they had managed to confiscate. But any attack was premature. More manpower and weapons were needed. Information about the enemies strength and position were needed. It would take another 36 hours to get everything into place. However, they could send a Blackhawk helicopter in to knock out the TV tower. This was done at once, and all broadcasting was stopped. Only the cable network was still in place.

March 15: National Guard from Tennessee, Southern Indiana and Illinois joined the Kentuckians along with reserves, ROTC, and all survivors from Ft. Campbell. This would be a tough battle. There were many civilians in and around Louisville. Governor Willis tried to get the word out to evacuate the city, but communications were limited. Today retired Colonel Jacoby took over command of the combined forces around Louisville. He had only been retired six months, and retired when he was passed over for promotion to Maj. General. He was a battle-tested soldier from the Gulf Wars. He laid out a plan to divide the enemy by taking the intersection of I-264 and I-65, and spread along I-264. So the main force came in from the east along the I-64 corridor, then to I-264 corridor. A smaller force under the command of Colonel Howard came from the south along the I-65 corridor.

Col. Jacoby's group crossed the outer perimeter of I-265 at 8:30 a.m. CST. The Chinese had scouts set up on every side of the city, and so Col. Jacoby's group was beset by a bombardment of ground-to-ground missiles. S.Sgt. O'Reiley had managed to round up some missiles himself. A couple of these were fired at the incoming missiles, with limited success. However, the tanks were equipped with an anti missile rapid fire systems that were successful. Although the tanks were successful in warding off any hits, still some landed among the Hummers and other vehicles. More than 1,000 American service men and women were killed in the first wave. But fight back they did. Missiles were launched onto the airport and at the now occupied National Guard Armory. Then came a wave of older Air Guard F16s out of Ohio. After about an hour of intense fighting, the enemy's missile attack stopped altogether. Col. Jacoby and his group gained possession of the I-264 corridor before noon, and split the Chinese into two groups.

Col. Howard and his group attacked the airport from the south at 2:00 p.m., by first sending in a wave of helicopters, followed by artillery. The helicopters met very little resistance. Evidently the combination of the F16s and the missile attack from Col. Jacoby's group had really taken their toll on the Chinese. By 4:00 p.m. tanks were rolling onto airport property. At first they were met with some shoulder launched missiles. Only two tanks were hit. As they came nearer the control tower, the Chinese had obviously given up the battle. At about 5:30 p.m.

a white flag appeared, and the battle was over.

After communicating this to Col. Jacoby, Col. Howard set up a temporary stockade to hold the Chinese prisoners and a field hospital to tend the wounded from both sides. Both groups settled in for the night. Tomorrow the concentration would be toward downtown Louisville. The American toll for the day was: 1557 dead, five tanks destroyed, two F-16s downed, one helicopter, and several smaller vehicles disabled or totaled. The Chinese lost 2986 personnel along with a host of missiles and transport planes.

March 14: The day started early, with everyone fed and ready to go by 6:00 a.m. This would be a much harder military maneuver. There were still at large number of civilians scattered across Louisville, plus the exact position of the enemy forces was hard to determine. Helicopters were ordered in first for a fly over at 2,000 feet. While flying over the entire downtown area, not one missile was fired at the helicopters. Next they went down to 1,000 feet. Still, no enemy fire. Now they went in at 500 feet or just 100 feet above the buildings. They drew no enemy fire.

Cautiously Col. Jacoby ordered his group to advance up I-65 and the parallel streets. His group was spread out over a path two miles wide. Very slowly they advanced northward. When they crossed Eastern Parkway, some citizens came out of buildings with flags flying, and a lot of cheering. Col. Jacoby would have none of it. He ordered Lt. Holmes, his attache, to make public address announcements for all citizens to take cover.

No resistance was met until they were passing Spalding University. Then it was a single shoulder-launched missile from a tall building. It struck the ground in front of a tank proceeding up 3rd St. A squad was ordered to go into the building, and secure it. Eventually they found only a single Chinese soldier. By this time it was 3:00 p.m. Rather than to risk attacking the downtown area at night and endangering many civilians, Col. Jacoby ordered everyone to take up defensive positions until the next morning.

March 15: Once again all personnel were ready by 6:00 a.m. The sun was not yet up, but the city center must be taken today. Once again the group advanced northward. Sgt. O'Reiley passed his boyhood home this morning. There was no activity inside. By noon the advance group was in sight of the City Hall. What they observed was a white flag flying. A Hummer was sent in with a white flag. No shots were fired. The approximately 2,000 Chinese soldiers had holed up in the City Hall and surrounding public buildings. Two unarmed soldiers were sent in to investigate. They were allowed inside the building. When they came back out, they had a message for Col. Jacoby. The Chinese had more than 200 hostages, and wanted safe conduct back the airport. Wow!!

Col. Jacoby gladly sent the two back in with a message: "Come out unarmed and you will be safely escorted to the airport to join your comrades." After about an hour of talking and arguing among themselves, they came out without any obvious arms. Immediately they were searched. Then they marched about seven miles to the airport and put in the temporary stockade. **The Battle of Louisville ended with a whimper.** The celebration lasted all night, then martial law was enforced with a dusk to dawn curfew. Tomorrow supplies would be allowed into the city, and other citizens would be allowed back into their homes.

CHAPTER 15

THE CRUISE SHIP WONDER OF THE CARRIBEAN

Lewis and Naomi Smith were on the cruise ship Wonder of the Carribean which was docked in Kingston, Jamaica. On the morning of the 11th the news of the attack on America had started coming in. Around 11:00 a.m., a fully armed cutter, flying the Cuban flag pulled alongside. With guns blazing, they came aboard the ship. After a brief fight with the ship's personnel, the Cubans took over. They wanted everyone put ashore, except some officers of the ship. The Cubans were vicious. After it appeared that not everyone was willing to obey their commands, they proceeded to individual cabins. In the cabin next door to the Smiths, the couple was killed in cold blood, when they stopped to pick up some extra clothing. Each person was forced to give up all money and possessions. Jamaica now had an extra 2,000 homeless and penniless people. Lewis and

Naomi went to the American Embassy, along with hundreds of others. The embassy had no way to cope. The embassy was already in shambles when they had heard the terrible news from home. All the passengers were assembled outside the embassy and told the news of the attack on America. Lewis and Naomi were dazed. They lived in Cincinnati. As far as they knew, their home, family and friends were no more. Lewis had a brother living near Nashville, Tn. Maybe they could contact them. Meanwhile, they had no means to take care of themselves. The embassy calmly took everyone's names and assigned them a number. It would take days to process everyone and give each person an opportunity to try and contact family or friends. Fortunately, Lewis had always had the motto: *Always be ready for a disaster.* In each of his shoes was a $100.00 bill. This might help take care of the two of them for a day or two. The goal: Find cheap lodging and food and maybe a change of clothing. It might be a while before they saw home again. He tried the nearest bank, to change his money into local currency. No luck. The bank was demanding a terrible exchange rate, in light of the recent events.

Slowly Lewis and Naomi realized that they were homeless vagrants in a hostile environment. That night they slept on the street, next to the embassy with hundreds of others. They were filled with fear for their own survival and terrible anxiety about their friends and family. Together they faced the greatest test of their lives. Hadn't they saved for retirement? Didn't they work hard to provide for their family, and didn't they give generously to church and other charities? All of that was behind them now. This would be one step at a time. It was a time for prayer. The next morning, Lewis and Naomi, invited all the people on the street with them, to join in a time of prayer. The primary focus of the prayer time was for America. Most realized that they may be among the fortunate Americans. Somehow they would return back to the United States, and start over. They would help with the war effort. So with renewed energy they set out to find food and shelter. Whatever each had, they would share with the others. "Give us this day our daily bread."

March 15: Today another cruise ship made a stop in Jamaica, and offered to take the *Wonder of the Carribean's* passengers to another port. The continental United States was out of the question, but would take them to Puerto Rico. This was accepted. On March 17, they arrived in San Juan, with a great welcome. Housing and food were in short demand, but the Puerto Ricans went all out to find places for everyone. Lewis and Naomi were placed in the home of Georgio and Louisa Garcia. They had five *niños* (children). With a little high school Spanish and the Garcia's English, communication took place, but sometimes mistakes were made. But it was all taken in good spirits. Lewis and Naomi stayed here until late April, when they could arrange transportation home.

Lewis and Naomi finally received news about Cincinnati. It was not good. The entire city had been blown up. But the Americans were counter attacking, and the Chinese had forgotten about the Naval base in Puerto Rico. Mostly, this part of the Navy was assigned to attack Cuba. The idea was to occupy Cuba, so that they would spend their energy on defense instead of sending soldiers into America. They had attacked and destroyed the Cuban Navy, and sent some air support to Ft. Lauderdale. They did launch one nuclear tipped missile into Havana. Most of Havana was destroyed. Otherwise they just occupied Cuba with random shelling of military sites, until such time as a coordinated strike could begin.

CHAPTER 16
MARCH 14 (TAIWAN TIME) INITIAL ATTACK ON CHINA

In the Taiwan Strait, the United States finally had two of the X Class submarines (the Rhode Island & the Dallas) in place. The Chinese had not detected their presence. The orders were opened. Sink every Chinese ship in the Strait, immediately. Captain Blake of the Rhode Island, realizing the gravity of the situation, obeyed immediately. Captain Finihas on the Dallas also obeyed. All torpedoes were activated, and the ships' positions calculated precisely, via satellite and listening devices. The two ships fired on the four closest ships. The ships went down. Next they would reposition to attack the rest. Before the day was over, 26 Chinese ships went to the bottom of the Taiwan Strait. The elation on the island of Taiwan was unbelievable. Evidently, the Chinese had chosen not to invade Taiwan. Perhaps they were just waiting for the collapse of America, after which time Taiwan would have to surrender.

Next set of orders: Destroy the Military Base of Chouwoo near Guangzhou, without hitting Hong Kong. And fire a hydrogen bomb warhead-tipped missile on Wuhan. The mission was carried out flawlessly. Had the Chinese miscalculated the strength of the American military, or the resolve of the American people? The two subs quietly disappeared into the Pacific. They would have to rearm from a sub supply ship.

Meanwhile in Korea, the Koreans and Americans, had a few nuclear missiles left over. The guidance systems were recalculated to strike Changchun, the Wandoo base (just north of the Yellow River) and one longer range missile with Beijing in its sights. General Barton (Commanding General of the American forces in Korea) requested permission to send four missiles into China. The Pentagon quickly gave permission for the launch. That would free up the ICBMs to strike military targets.

By the time the Chinese realized that the ships in the Taiwan Strait, were being sunk, a nuclear missile had struck the Wandoo base. The missiles aimed at Changchun did not strike the city, but did explode outside in the country side. The problem was hard to pinpoint. Faulty guidance systems, long inactive rocket engines, or maybe good Chinese anti missile systems were all possibilities. It would take some analysis of the data from the launch, and no one had time for that right now. The long range missile aimed at Beijing also missed the mark, but still exploded about 25 miles from the center of the city. This would probably do great damage to a large part of Beijing. The Chinese now knew they were in for a fight.

CHAPTER 17
FIRE IN THE SKY

The Chinese Premier, Tau Yua, now realized that more must be done. He ordered the launch of a dozen long range missiles of the Woh class. These would be able to reach the continental United States. On March 13, after the nuclear explosion above Beijing, the twelve missiles were launched.

They were detected almost immediately, by American satellites. The anti missile sites were immediately put on alert. Prepare all defensive missiles for a launch. But the Chinese missiles seemed to be going haywire. Four were launched to the Southeast, away from America. Would China actually attack South America or Australia? The Australians were very alarmed. The others were dispersed over an arc toward Thailand, India, the Middle East, and Africa. Had the guidance systems gone completely haywire?

It was not until the first exploded over Sumatra at 22,238 miles above the equator, that the intelligence organizations of the world knew what was happening. It was going to be an attempt to disrupt communications worldwide. If a satellite was not hit directly, the radiation from the nuclear explosion would probably affect nearly every satellite in a geosynchronous orbit. The explosions occurred with split second precision, over most of the equator. The display was awesome. It was dark over South America, and Africa when the explosions came. The night sky was lit up over thousands of miles.

Also the navigational satellites with GPS capabilities would be disabled or destroyed. Almost every ship and airplane built within the last 25 years was equipped to use this type of navigation. In addition many airports, trucks, and cars had this capability. All the U.S. Army, Navy, Air Force and Coast Guard vessels were equipped with GPS as the primary navigational tool. Many missiles depended upon this for the primary positional technology. That is, this is how they determined exactly where they were during a flight. Although all military vehicles were equipped with alternative navigational instruments, this would make things more difficult. Some might get into the wrong position, which might cause allies to shoot at the wrong target. Also, missiles could fail to hit the exact mark. The Chinese seemed to understand the importance of disrupting the allies' communicatins and navigation.

The United States military satellites were

prepared for this scenario. Just before the first explosion, Col. Joe Mustedo, of the Air Force ordered all intelligence satellites shut down and put into a nuclear hardened shell. A direct hit would kill a satellite, but the radiation would not. It would be a waiting game, now. How soon would the radiation decrease enough that the satellites could be put back into working order? Joe had been prepared for this for a long time. He relayed the information back to the Pentagon (most of whom were working out of the mountains of Colorado). He made two suggestions: "Wait until the radiation decreases, and try one satellite at a time. Also, immediately put up as many intelligence satellites as possible into a different orbit. This would keep these satellites out of the radiation." Even though Cape Kennedy had been destroyed, we could launch satellites from Vandenberg Air Force Base in California (which had been spared a direct hit). Also Redstone Arsenal in North Alabama, was still in the missile business. It would take a minimum of twenty-four hours and possibly longer to prepare a launch site from one of the old test stands. The people of Huntsville and surrounding cities would understand the necessity. In addition the Navy claimed that a submarine could launch a satellite into orbit.

A Chinese submarine also went after the undersea cables laid across the Atlantic Ocean. They were successful in cutting one cable, but the Submarine Bush attacked and destroyed the sub before any more damage could be done. Minimal communications were still possible with our European allies.

Meanwhile, what were the Chinese up to that they needed to stop communications? They had to know that most of the military satellites were not in a geosynchronous orbit.

When the next spy satellite approached China, another rocket roared into the night air. The Chinese would try to destroy any satellite coming over their territory. Joe Mustedo ordered the shut down of this one, too. If it did not take a direct hit, it would be out of the radiation within an hour and back in service. But, of course, our military depended on some of the geosynchronous satellites to communicate back with the ground. That is, they were not always over a ground communications point, but were always in range of the geosynchronous satellites or a ground station and usually in range of another spy satellite. Therefore, getting instant information from our military satellites might be difficult. Capt. Howie Holton suggested to Col. Mustedo that we fly some of the old spy planes out over the Pacific, and set up a link, outside of Chinese anti missile defense system, but where the spy satellites could make contact. The idea was forwarded to the Pentagon and a decision was made to put at least two of the planes into service, but this would take a few days to properly outfit the planes, and bring them up to proper working order.

Because of the new situation, the President, Jake Oderon, decided to launch a full scale nuclear attack on China. He did not know if all the bombs would explode or not. Many were very old. It was possible that some had deteriorated and would not explode, but there was no time to fully check every warhead. Every sub not engaged in hunting down the Chinese subs or ships, was ordered to get within striking distance of China. All operable long range bombers with air to ground missiles were equipped with nuclear warheads. France and Great Britain were consulted, and both agreed to participate with their own nuclear weapons. This was communicated to China. If the fight did not stop within forty-eight hours, China would be destroyed. Estimates for Chinese dead from such an attack were put at 150 to 500 million. Also, the radiation from such an attack would destroy most of China's agricultural lands.

CHAPTER 18
CHINA'S ANSWER

arch 15, 15 hours after the ultimatum from the United States and her allies: China's answer came loud and clear. A Chinese sub surfaced off Santa Catalina Island. Two missiles were launched. Both were aimed at the China Lake Naval Weapons Center, where it was suspected that America stored a number of nuclear warheads. The Navy did have some Patriot missiles guarding the site. One met the first missile over the Mojave Desert, where the nuclear explosion took place. The second missile was camouflaged somewhat by the first explosion, and made it to the target. The area north of Ridgecrest, California, was destroyed. The sub was tracked down and destroyed.

Unexpectedly, the tremors from the attack on China Lake evidently struck some underground rock formations and caused some shaking of Hoover Dam. Several cracks developed. An alarm was sounded to evacuate all cities and towns below the dam. The chief engineer on duty, Kristin Foberty, ordered the lowering of the water as fast as possible. Two hours later the dam began to crumble. In minutes the great dam dissolved into debris. The evacuation below the dam was too slow. Bullhead City, Arizona, and Laughlin, Nevada were hit first. Down the river to Needles, California the flood came. There had not been enough time to properly evacuate. The I 40 bridge at Topoch, Arizona, was knocked out. Lake Huvasu City, Arizona was hit next. The area around Blythe, California had some extra time and managed to evacuate, but the I 10 bridge was destroyed. Yuma, Arizona also had time to do mass evacuation, as did the cities of Gadsden and San Luis in Mexico. Now another problem had to be dealt with. The remaining population in Southern California had no supply of clean water. The water from the aqueducts from Northern California would have to be checked for radiation before it could be used.

A second sub surfaced in the English Channel. Two missiles were also fired, one toward Paris, France the other toward London, England. Neither made it to the intended target, but both did explode over France and England. The Chinese sub never had the chance to launch another missile. Aerial and naval attacks were almost instantaneous. Captain Richards of the RAF had been assigned to patrol the Channel and was the first to launch an air-to-ground missile. The British Navy and the French Air Force followed up. This sub would never cause another problem for the allies.

The answer from China was very clear. The attack would go forward, but with great regret. How much of the world would be destroyed before this war stopped? It was expected that it would be late in the day of March 17 on the Chinese coast before everything would be in place. That would be at about 5:00 a.m. in the Rocky Mountains, and mid day in Europe. What else would China try before that time?

By this time most of China's navies were lying beneath the sea. What else were they going to try? Where was their massive army? About three hundred thousand had actually invaded the United States, and, except for the forces in and around Sacramento and on the coast around Monterey, all were either destroyed, captured or engaged in actual combat where they had little chance of success. Where were the rest of the 50 - 100 million soldiers?

CHAPTER 19
REDSTONE ARSENAL AND MARSHALL SPACEFLIGHT CENTER IN NORTH ALABAMA

Redstone Arsenal was located near Huntsville, Alabama, north of the Tennessee River. It was originally a munitions storage facility, but with strong congressional support, it had become a missile research center. In fact, the leading German missile scientists from Germany had been sent here after World War II. In the 1950s the rockets developed here were so good that one of them had launched America's first satellite. With that launch, it was decided to carve out a NASA base on the Arsenal. Thus, Marshall Spaceflight Center was born. Most of the large rockets for America's space programs were born here. Also, the Arsenal was still in the business of developing rockets and missiles for the U.S. Army. This was an obvious target for the Chinese.

Linda Baker awakened with a start that morning of March 11. Something was different, but what was it? It was only 5:00 a.m. She wasn't due at work until 8:00 a.m. Maybe she was imagining things. She just lay there thinking about the past year. One year . . . A year ago she had a husband and three wonderful children. She was totally involved in motherhood. The boys, Nick and Hal, were ten and six and Susan was eight. All were in school, and George, her husband, had a good job on the Arsenal with a contractor. "Could it be only a year?" she thought.

Last March 20, George had come in with an announcement. He took Linda aside and said, "I've fallen in love with someone. I'm packing my bags and going to live with her. I'm sorry." "He was sorry.", she thought. "He never gave a single thought about me and the kids. He was only thinking about that thing between his legs, that's all." Three months later the divorce was made final. George promised full child support, which he paid occasionally. Linda had to find work. She had a degree in business, and had taken several computer programming courses, so she headed to Redstone Arsenal personnel office. There she found an opening as an electronics instructor, if she was able to complete some courses herself. So she was hired within the month. She studied hard, but work and motherhood together were hard. She had to put her children in an after school program. She really missed the time with them, but she managed to keep everything going.

She did like the work. She was assigned to teach maintenance on the new Patriot X missiles. She was good at this, which surprised her. Her understanding of the systems and the software seemed to come naturally. After a few months, she noticed that the launch program seemed to be slower than seemed necessary. One day when things were a bit slow, she decided to look at the program a little more. What seemed a little more turned into a part time study over the next month. Finally she decided to enter her new version of the program into a simulator. It worked except for a small glitch. The next day she corrected the glitch, and launched the program with the simulator. It was not only faster, but it checked more items! She was absolutely thrilled. However she knew the bureaucracy well enough that she could not make the suggestion by herself.

And so she reminisced about how to approach her bosses with this suggestion until 6:00 a.m. when she knew that the day must start. Three children fed and off to school. Then she had to drive out to the Arsenal to her job. No time to dally. It was March 11. **That Day!**

At the training center she was in a classroom at 10:00 a.m. when the explosion rocked the building. Her first thought was an accident. Maybe one of the rockets had exploded? But she learned that it was not an accident, and that it was happening all over America. The classes were dismissed early, and everyone was instructed to seek a good shelter for the night. There might be a lot of radiation. She picked up her children as soon as she could and headed home. She did notice that the winds were blowing toward the southeast, moving the radioactive clouds away from Huntsville.

On March 11, a nuclear bomb had exploded south of the Tennessee River, obviously missing its intended target. Most of the 20,000 workers on the Arsenal and Spaceflight Center were at work when the bomb exploded at 10:00 a.m. CST. The Arsenal was protected by some Patriot missiles, and the radar did detect the incoming missile. However, a lone missile, traveling at about two thousand miles per hour, was thought to be a glitch in the system and no Patriot was launched.

No one was allowed to go to work the next day unless they were summoned. Schools were out. But on March 13, she and most other employees of the Arsenal were ordered back to work. Once there she found out that the classes were going to be suspended for a while. Some of the instructors were going to be assigned other jobs. It seemed that Kennedy Spaceflight Center had been destroyed, and Marshall Spaceflight Center and U.S. Army personnel were going to launch some missiles from right here. Linda was assigned to a unit that was making the Patriot rockets into rockets that would launch satellites.

They were asked to work twelve hour shifts. She would have to ask some of her neighbors to help out. Marlene and Frank Jones were a retired couple just a couple doors away, and they volunteered with the comment, "We must all pull together in this time of emergency."

As excited as she was about the challenge, she was also very concerned about her children. She did every dirty job she was asked to do. She did have a pretty good understanding about the electronics, but no one asked her for any input. When she had time she liked to continue studying the machine language program which had been designed for the Patriot launch. It was just an extension of the program she had been exploring before **That Day.** Linda knew a better way to assemble the program. The next question she asked herself was, "Will anyone listen to me?" On the third day, March 16, they thought they had the system ready. They put it through a simulation. Failure! Finally, everyone was called together, and the bosses asked everyone for their ideas on what would make this thing fly with the new payload. Linda spoke up. She went over to one of the computers and opened the program, and went right to the point where she thought there was a glitch. Quickly she corrected it in machine language. A few said that she could not possibly know enough to make a program like that work, but others decided that they had nothing to lose. Time was very important. The United States needed to replace lost satellites now! The simulation was run again with success. The engineers and scientists were absolutely amazed. A beefed up Patriot would launch a satellite that night. The launch window was open between 9:00 and 11:00 p.m.

Even though Linda was due home at 7:00 p.m., she stayed but made a call to the Jones' house to see about her children. The launch went perfectly. Everyone cheered when the rocket lifted off an old test stand. A little later word was received that the satellite was in orbit, and with a few corrections, was sending data back to earth. More cheering!! But tomorrow would be another challenge. More satellites must be put up. For now, at least, Linda was a heroine. She downplayed her input, correctly pointing out that people smarter than her had put the program together. Others had put the extra rockets in place, still others had designed the Patriot. Others made the satellite. Still, she was something of a celebrity, and liked the status.

Also, she was now a solid part of the programming team and felt that her input would help get America going again.

CHAPTER 20
TAKES TIME TO LAUNCH A COORDINATED ATTACK

March 16 in Europe

President Oderon, Prime Minister Baker of Great Britain, President Du Jacques of France, Chancellor Schmidt of Germany, President Ferraz of Spain, President Ciampi of Italy, Prime Minister Jagon of Japan, Prime Minister George of Australia and Prime Minister Williams of Canada met in Geneva, Switzerland. Forty-eight hours would not be enough time to coordinate an all-out attack against China. It would have to wait until the 20th or just hit China piecemeal. Which way would put China out of business the quickest? On the seventeenth, Russia's President, Kostar, came to the meeting. Russia had decided to join the allies' effort to crush China. It seems that about half a million Chinese soldiers were poised along the Chinese-Russian border.

The discussions went on a long time with experts from many fields joining the arguments about how best to destroy China. If China was to be hit with one bomb at a time, would that embolden the Chinese with the idea that the allies did not have enough weapons to destroy China? Therefore China could immediately launch all out attacks wherever she pleased. Or would the delay in getting all the pieces in place cause China to do the same. Or maybe allow Russia to strike China with an all-out nuclear attack, followed by the rest of the allies a day or two later? By the morning of the 18th a plan had been devised. An all-out attack on the 20th was decided. The time for the launch of the first missiles was scheduled for 10.00 a.m. Now the President waited. China had massed troops not only along Russia's border, but also along the border with Myanmar (Burma) and along the border with Kazakhstan.

In Korea, the forces of Korea, United States, and (amazingly) Japan, were preparing to cross into China. (Korea had not trusted Japan since the occupation more than a century ago, which ended in 1945 at the end of World War II, but here they were side by side.)

CHAPTER 21
THE SUDDEN CHANGE : MARCH 19

About midnight (MST) on the 18th, President Oderon was informed of a shift in troop position along the Russian border. At 2:10 a.m. on the 19th (MST, 5:10 p.m. in Beijing), a report from the Myanmar border stated that the Chinese troops seemed to be in disarray. Some appeared to be retreating from the border; others were advancing into Myanmar. In the west, on the border of Kazakhstan, there was no evidence of any Chinese troops. It looked like the army simply disappeared. The President had to wait until the next satellite passed over the region at 3:15 a.m. MST (5:15 p.m. local time in western China). All the leaders of the allies had been informed. Meanwhile, the all-out attack on China was scheduled for 6:00 a.m. March 20, Beijing time. From the satellite overflight to launch is about 12 hours. There must be time to analyze the data.

There has been no response from China since the missile attack on France, Great Britain, and

China Lake, California. Then, at 6:30 p.m. in Beijing, came a startling message, *"The oppressors of the former government of China have been overthrown. Premier On and fellow believers in democracy have taken over the government. All hostilities toward other countries will be stopped at once. China has no desire to dominate the world."* They were so few words, but it held such great promise. Or was it just a trick to delay the attack on China?

President Oderon and the allies decided to delay the all-out attack on China while awaiting further news. This announcement from China was a verification of the information from the satellite – the troops had withdrawn from the Kazakhstan border. A meeting of the United Nations would convene in Geneva[2] as soon as most of the nations could get representatives in place. The Russian embassy in Beijing was still intact. The Ambassador would have to verify the new status until the Allies could set up some communications. Meanwhile, the hawks around the U.S.A. were demanding that the full scale attack should continue against China. America had been dealt a severe blow, and many wanted revenge. Nothing less than the destruction of China would suffice. The Church leaders, who had survived, advised delaying the attacks until more information could be

---

[2] The U.N. Building in New York had been severely damaged in the nuclear attack.

acquired. The former U.S. Ambassador to China, Lucius Wentworth, who spoke excellent Mandarin, was called into action, and placed on a plane heading to Tianjin, to meet with Chinese officials there. (The condition of the Airport in Beijing was unknown.) Ambassador Wentworth had some specific questions that had to be answered: Will American troops be allowed on Chinese soil to determine if China is truly surrendering? Will China give aid to America for the rebuilding of our country?

The questions on the table for President Oderon were: Did China now want peace? Or had they realized that the United States of America and her allies were still able to launch great destruction upon China? Even if China wants peace, were we willing to negotiate a peace with so much of our country destroyed? Would anything other than unconditional surrender suffice? Would destroying China serve any purpose other than revenge?

CHAPTER 22
THE MEETING IN CHINA MARCH 21

After a very tedious trip, Lucius Wentworth arrived in what was left of Beijing. In the northern suburbs a capital had been set up. He met first with the Ambassador from Russia, Mikhail Worsky. During the long meeting, it became evident that the Russians wanted to destroy China or at least occupy most of the country. Also Ambassador Worsky believed that the Chinese were without sincerity about the change in government. He believed that the change was a mere pretense to stop or delay the attack on China. However, there were new leaders. A Central Committee had been formed to rule over the country until such time as a public election could be held. Premier On appeared to be the spokesperson for the group.

March 22 Ambassador Wentworth was scheduled to meet with the Central Committee at 10:00 a.m. Beijing time. The Central Committee had 34 members. Much of the time was spent in establishing protocol. It seemed that the Chinese leaders were not of one voice. This would make negotiations very difficult. However, the Central Committee did state that an election would be set up in the near future. It would take a lot of organization and time to have a meaningful election. To the question of having outside monitors observing the election, there were mixed replies. A few agreed, but some wanted more time to discuss this, and some were adamant that no foreigner's observers would be allowed. The ones with the strongest objection stated that China was now the strongest military nation on earth and would not allow any foreign interference. Ambassador Wentworth finally stated, "One order of business should be taken care of right now. What are you going to do about the Chinese troops stationed on American soil? Can we cease all hostilities until such time as we can reach some agreement?"

Premier On answered, "If we agree to this, will you be able to stop your armed forces from attacking our troops?"

Ambassador Wentworth, "President Oderon has agreed to do just that. But at some point your troops will need to lay down their arms and be escorted to China. How soon can you communicate with your forces?"

Premier On, "It will take some time. Can we agree in principle and discuss the exact timing tomorrow? We will need to discuss this situation with our military leaders."

Ambassador Wentworth, "I will ask President Oderon to put our troops in a defensive position for twenty-four hours. If you can get your troops into only a defensive position within that time, then we can discuss the other matters tomorrow. Colonel Harmon of the U.S. Army will be present tomorrow to discuss this matter in more detail with your Army. "

With that the meeting ended abruptly.

March 23. Today, Ambassador Wentworth stated the obvious, "We have received no indication that your troops stationed on American soil have stopped all hostilities. In fact the force in and around Central California are continuing to move outward. This is an intolerable situation."

Premier On, "It has been difficult to communicate with these soldiers. They were given preliminary instruction to not listen to any outside orders until they joined up with other Chinese forces on the coast. We will try again."

Ambassador Wentworth stated, "That makes for a very difficult situation. How can we negotiate peace, if your soldiers are still conducting offensive maneuvers on our soil?"

Ambassador Wentworth continued, "The armed forces of The United States and her allies must be allowed into China or China will face nuclear doom. Also, China must disarm." Some of the Central Committee were furious. After all, the belief was that the United States had been destroyed, and could not deliver on such a threat. Further China had withdrawn its troops from all the foreign borders, and posed no threats to any other country. Ambassador Wentworth was asked to leave until the Central Committee could provide a definitive answer.

March 24. Ambassador Wentworth communicated the problems back to President Oderon, and he passed the information to the allies. He was not able to talk with the Central Committee today. He did speak to the Russian ambassador who requested that he be allowed to attend any future talks. This was agreed upon.

March 25. The British and French ambassadors arrived, but no talks were scheduled. However, the Taiwan government now wanted a spokesperson in any future meetings. This was getting out of hand.

March 26. Finally a meeting was scheduled. The American, Russian, British and French ambassadors went together. When they arrived, only the Russian and American Ambassadors were allowed into the meeting. Upon entering it was quickly noted that there were only 14 members of the Central Committee in attendance. Ambassador Wentworth asked the obvious question. Premier On was not present. The spokesperson for the Chinese was Had Waong. Waong answered the questions curtly. "The other members are gathering data from the different provinces and will not be able to attend any more meetings. Further, a recess to the talks is requested until such time as more information from the provinces can be gathered."

Ambassador Wentworth stated that this was impossible. "Even now many in the West are ready to launch an all-out attack against China. If immediate concessions are not received then I have no authority to stop such an attack. The United States has been dealt a severe blow which killed more than fifty million. Many want revenge, but all want China to agree to disarm and allow monitors to observe this process. A long delay is not going to be allowed. The United States and her allies will destroy China if no immediate agreement is forthcoming. You have forty-eight hours to respond. Furthermore, representatives from the other countries and Taiwan will be allowed to attend any additional talks.

"One other problem exists. You have troops on the ground in America who are now fighting and killing our troops and holding our citizens captive. Can you communicate with them? If so, will you order them to cease hostilities. If you give such an order and they stop hostilities then our president will stop all military actions against them. At our next meeting we can determine what to do with your troops who are now on our land." The meeting ended abruptly. The Chinese walked out without commenting on Ambassador Wentworth's statement. They appeared to be in a huff.

The four ambassadors returned to their hotels. They consulted briefly to consider their options. The first decision was where could they go to discuss this turn privately? They decided to return to Tiajin and board the British transport which had brought Ambassador Sterling.

March 27. The Chinese Central Committee requested a meeting through the Russian embassy. The meeting was scheduled for 3:00 p.m. This time there were five members which included the representative from Taiwan, Choung Waer. All were allowed to enter the room where the talks were to take place.

Had Woang opened the meeting. The Chinese were willing to reduce the size of the military and allow a representative from a neutral nation to observe this process.

Choung Waer from Taiwan answered for everyone, "This answer is totally inadequate. China has no navy and cannot prevent an attack from the outside. Further the Chinese have used all the available nuclear weapons and long range missiles in the initial attack. The only military resources available to China are the very large armies. Any concentrated attack against any other nation will receive a nuclear answer. The troops will simply be annihilated. China started the nuclear war and every nuclear power on earth is now willing to use nuclear retaliation against China. This includes China's neighbors of Pakistan, India and Russia in addition to the United States of America, Great Britain and France. A great host of nuclear bombs will rain down on China if she refuses to disarm and allow inspection of the disarmament on Chinese soil by representatives of the nations which China attacked. Brothers, I beg you to reconsider.

"The people of Taiwan want to unite with Central China and form a freely elected government. We can help with this process. We do not want to rule over China. Truly, the task of ruling over such a great nation would be very difficult. But it is not too large a job to destroy the military and industrial complexes spread across China. Nuclear bombs could annihilate the industrial factories of China, the military sites and plants, and the fallout of radiation across China would kill millions and create a wasteland of the agricultural lands.

"Most of the forty-eight hours which were granted to you have already been used. Even now submarines with nuclear missiles have gathered off your coast. All nuclear tipped missile batteries in the United States, France, Great Britain, and Russia are on full alert. Airplanes loaded with air to ground nuclear missiles are in the air. I beg of you to disarm and give permission for full inspection. If you refuse and China is destroyed, it is not this group of people who will rule over China. The allies will install others and consider you the enemy."

The Chinese stood by the first offer, with no other conditions. Only a neutral nation could observe the disarmament.

CHAPTER 23

BACK IN THE UNITED STATES ON MARCH 21

With China now negotiating, President Oderon turned his thoughts inward toward regaining control of the country and helping the starving and sick people. John Taylor gave a full report on the status of the American people. Clean water was almost impossible to obtain in and around the large cities where a nuclear explosion had taken place. Food supplies could not be delivered with any expedience, because of the destruction of the highway system and railroads. Even in places like Atlanta and Denver, where no nuclear explosion took place, it was hard to deliver adequate supplies. The Supermarkets had run out of food by the end of March 13 and no new supplies were flowing in. Some riots had broken out when delivery trucks actually brought food in. So the National Guard and police forces were assigned to every truck with orders to shoot. However water was in good supply in each city and, indeed, they were shipping truckloads of water to other more needy places. Electricity had been restored to most places that did not take a direct hit, orders were given to use power sparingly.

In the places like Los Angeles, New York, Baltimore, San Francisco, Chicago, Miami, and the other cities where the nuclear explosions occurred the situation was much more desperate. No medical facilities were in operation to take care of the many wounded people and those exposed to radiation. A decision was made to take care of the wounded and desperately sick first. They were transported to the nearest city or community hospital where they could get assistance. For instance, most of the wounded and sick around Chicago were transported north to Wisconsin, where no nuclear explosion had taken place. Those suffering from radiation poisoning were placed in schools, motels, and community centers. Other than food and water, they had no care. The whole system was overwhelmed and priorities had to be set. The communities, where they were sent, were asked to care for these victims. But some places had no food or water to care for themselves, and thus these victims were at the bottom of the priority list. This was a tragedy so big and so awful that no one could effectively care for the victims.

President Oderon went begging to the countries where we had given great help. He asked that they send doctors, nurses, food, oil, and medicines. Some turned a cold ear to our problems, but some were more willing. Brazil, Canada, the European Union, South Africa, Mexico, Argentina, Australia, New Zealand, Japan, Israel, Pakistan, Russia and several smaller nations in Central America pledged to help. And so by the 23rd of March supplies were flowing into the United States. But one great problem hindered that. Most of our ports were destroyed. The smaller ports of Mobile, Alabama, Savannah, Georgia, Morro Bay, California, Wilmington, North Carolina, New Haven, Connecticut, and Astoria, Washington would have to take a big role in receiving and distributing the supplies. The Air National Guard transport squadrons were assigned to help distribute goods from Brazil and Australia. Other transportation groups in the National Guard were to help transport goods from the port cities. Wherever trains could run, they were given priorities to distribute food and water first, then deliver gas and oil. Coal deliveries to the power plants around the country also received a high priority. Executives of UPS, FEDEX, and other air freight companies were put in charge of the transportation of essential supplies of medicine and critical materials to keep essential industry running. Trucking company executives were given commissions in the Army and given command over the distribution of goods to small and large cities alike.

One big problem still existed: Sacramento, California was in the hands of about 200,000 Chinese troops. Even after the change of government in China on the 19th, these Chinese troops did not want to give up their stronghold. In fact, they were still expanding their area of control. Almost every American had fled the area. A few were being held hostage, and a few others were needed to run certain utilities and stores. By now, a ring of Nike EXs, Army antiaircraft missiles, had been moved close enough that no other airplanes could fly into the airport. So the Chinese troops were cut off from further reinforcement. But they refused to surrender and were now opening a front which appeared to be heading toward Santa Rosa and the coast. Apparently, their orders were to fight to the death, so that China could emerge victorious as the greatest superpower on Earth.

What were the options? One, simply wait. Maybe the news from China would dishearten them and they would surrender. Two, attack with whatever troops could be rounded up for this purpose. Three, drop a neutron bomb on the city. This bomb would kill almost everyone in a nine-mile radius, and leave almost no radiation and no buildings would be destroyed.

All three options had significant problems. Waiting was bad because the Chinese were conducting raids and gradually expanding the territory they controlled. An attack would result in a huge loss of life for the U.S. and China. The Chinese were well armed and had a few fighter planes and several advanced helicopters. The neutron bomb would kill many innocent Americans trapped behind the Chinese lines.

But, probably, an attack on the Chinese would result in the loss of more than 10,000 American troops. There were only a few hundred Americans left in the central city area. And waiting had already resulted in several hundred being killed as they resisted the Chinese.

CHAPTER 24
THE DECISION FOR SACRAMENTO

On March 24, President Oderon convened a meeting of his top level advisors: Secretary of State Joslyn Ohman , Secretary of Defense Jack Peremba, Director of Homeland Security John Taylor, Chairman of the Armed Forces Admiral Kerry Eubanks, Speaker of the House Joseph Lewis, Minority Leader of the Senate Young Son, Personal Advisor to the President, Julie Gonzalez and Vice President Lon Anderson.

The purpose of the meeting was to decide if dropping a neutron bomb on Sacramento was the right thing to do. But the meeting started with a briefing from Secretary of State Ohman. Joslyn updated the group about the negotiations that were ongoing in China. Particularly troublesome was the reluctance of China to discuss such critical problems as disarmament, inspections on Chinese soil, and the continuing battles on American soil.

Secretary of Defense Peremba updated the military situation. The United State military and the allies were still in position to launch an all-out attack on China. This position could not be maintained for a long period of time. The long range bombers had to return home on a regular basis for refueling, maintenance, and rest for the airmen. Some planes were being kept in position at all times for possible attack. Even the subs would need to return to base for restocking of supplies at some point. Right now we were in good shape to launch an attack, but a delay of a week would significantly weaken the ability to launch an all-out attack. But it could be resumed in waves.

The situation at home was addressed by John Taylor (Home Defense). "The battles in Wilmington, Delaware, Mobile, Alabama, Corpus Christie, Texas, Ft. Lauderdale, Florida, and Coos Bay, Oregon are over. All the foreign troops in these areas either are dead or being held in a prison. In California the situation is still going badly. The Chinese are not stopping their aggression. In Sacramento the Chinese have more than 200,000 troops in place. Along the coast near Salinas there is a large body of foreign troops advancing inland and except for some local resistance by National Guard and police forces this group is receiving no substantial opposition. The Army and Air Force are trying to get more of our forces in place. There are only 550,000 military personnel left in the United States. The rest are dead, injured, stationed overseas or involved in the attack on China. Most of these are being used for homeland security and the battles in other states. We are here to discuss our options. Listen to what Admiral Eubanks has to say."

Admiral Eubanks addressed the group with a polite introduction and then gave the startling possibilities. "For California these are the problems: We cannot get a substantial force in place for at least two weeks. If there are other outbreaks of hostilities against our country here or abroad, it will be delayed even more. Right now the Chinese are still congregated in Sacramento and along the coast. We don't know how long this situation will continue. They may start spreading out at any time. We do have Nike antiaircraft missiles close enough to stop any more aircraft from landing in Sacramento, and the Coast Guard is maintaining a close watch along the coast around Monterey in order to prevent any more landings by foreign troops.

"Our options are: One: Maintain the present position. The Chinese are killing a substantial number of our citizens each day because of our patriot citizens' opposition and refusal to cooperate. The willingness of our countrymen to carry on will probably wane with each succeeding day. Also, we can hope that the negotiations with the Chinese will motivate the Chinese troops to stop, and simply maintain their present positions. So far, we have no way of knowing of they can even communicate with their homeland. We have stopped trying to block their communications, in hope that some news from China will reach them. Our best guess is that they were given specific instructions to not believe any such news from home. Therefore, the Chinese will probably continue the attack on California.

"Option two: We have in our possession a nuclear device which can be exploded over an area which will kill all the people in a certain radius, without destroying the buildings. The radiation from this bomb has been shown to be the type that quickly dissipates, similar to a microwave oven. Particularly in Sacramento, this weapon would kill about 80% of the Chinese as they are now deployed. Also it would kill up to only about 1,000 Americans, but probably much less since the overwhelming majority of our citizens has evacuated the city. About the only ones still in the city are the ones that the Chinese are keeping under guard. On the coast the concentration of Chinese troops is not sufficient to make this a viable alternative.

"Ladies and Gentlemen, we have no other options. The failure to act quickly will probably result in the loss of more than the 10,000 civilians as the Chinese expand their territory, and an ensuing battle will cost us more than 10,000 American military casualties, when we can get them into place. You have a very difficult decision to make."

President Oderon responded, "Gentleman, we do have a very difficult decision. The Chinese are either unwilling to stop their troops in California, or unable to do it. If we choose to bomb our own country, it is unlikely that any of us will ever be elected to office again. If we don't, then a great many lives will be sacrificed for our careers. If any of you who are cabinet members choose not to go with us on this decision, then I suggest that you resign your post immediately. What say you?"

There were some mumbling and whispering, then Vice President Lon Anderson spoke, "I see no one handing in their resignation. What do we say?"

Then all spoke with one voice, "We are with you Mr. President!"

President Oderon, "Admiral Eubanks, you have your orders. I will give you written authority within the hour. How soon can you deliver the weapon?"

President Oderon added, "If the Chinese change their position, then we can change ours up to the time the bomb is dropped. Thank you, ladies and gentlemen, for your support. The history books will treat us with much dishonor, but we have made the correct decision."

Admiral Eubanks, "The bomb can be made

ready in one hour. Delivery will take up to three hours."

With that the meeting was adjourned. A far reaching and gut wrenching decision had been made. It was no longer a political decision, but a military one.

CHAPTER 25
THE BATTLES IN CALIFORNIA

At a site in the Southwestern United States, Captain Ron Witherspoon was awakened from a deep sleep and given the orders. He stood up to Colonel John Younis and spoke, "I have friends and family living in Sacramento. I won't do it!"

Col. Younis, "The facts are these: More than 10,000 American troops will lose their lives if we are to stop the attack by the Chinese. There will be many civilian casualties from the battle over Sacramento. On the other hand, there are only about 1,000 civilians left in Sacramento. The Chinese have 200,000 soldiers, of which 100,000 are concentrated near the airport. The bomb will kill everyone in a 2-mile radius, whether they are under cover or not. Most within a five-mile radius will die within a few days. Our intelligence people tell us that the Chinese will lose the majority of their forces before the end of the third day. Probably, the ranking officers will die at the time of detonation. Our hope is that the rest will give up the fight at that point. There will be very little physical damage to the city, and the radiation will dissipate very rapidly. Almost all buildings may be occupied within a week. This is our best hope to limit American casualties.

"Captain Witherspoon, you have your orders."

With reluctance, at 5:15 p.m. Sacramento time, Air Force Captain Ron Witherspoon took off in an S12, a plane that was invisible to radar. He flew from an undisclosed location with a ROT[3] air-to-ground missile that was also invisible to radar and armed with a Neutron Bomb. As he flew, he thought about his grandparents and the friends he had made while visiting them in Sacramento as a child. *How many would this bomb kill? When this is all over will everyone call him a traitor?* But he knew that he had his orders and any delay in the launch might give the Chinese time to disperse.

At 6:55 he approached the launch position above Carson City, Nevada. With final clearance from the President he pressed the launch button at 7:00 p.m. precisely. At 7:05 p.m., Sacramento time, the Bomb exploded above Sacramento. A nuclear device had been exploded above an American city by our own military. It was to become an issue that would reverberate through history.

March 25: Having been warned to take cover on the previous night, the forces defending

---

[3] ROT – Right on Target

central California were awakened with renewed awareness. Gen. R.T. Hollister of the National Guard had taken command of the combined forces, with units from the surrounding states of Oregon, Nevada, Arizona and even Idaho. From as far away as Alabama and Pennsylvania helicopters, and Air Guard fighters and bombers had been brought to California. He called together his staff and outlined what had happened and the strategy for the upcoming battles. He now had about 150,000 soldiers, sailors, airmen, and marines. The Chinese had about 200,000 around Sacramento and another 100,000 advancing inland from Monterey. He assigned Colonel Quentin Rodriguez and his group of about 30,000 the task of stalling the Chinese coming from Monterey.

After the news of the neutron bomb explosion over Sacramento, General Hollister decided to hold off any attack until March 26. This allowed time for the exposed Chinese to die. The decision seemed so cold to the General, but this was war. At daybreak two F-16s (now stationed in Redding, California) did a reconnaissance flight over the outskirts of the Chinese occupied area. No missiles were fired at either aircraft. The two ventured toward Sacramento, and again no missiles came their way. Finally, they bravely flew directly over Sacramento. There was no activity at all. Around noon a strike force advanced toward Sacramento from the town of Thermalito toward Yuba City, which was in the hands of the invaders. There was no resistance. When the force came into the city, the citizens who had remained in town, came out with a huge welcome.

With that much information, General Hollister ordered all forces to advance toward Sacramento, and to offer all enemy forces an opportunity to surrender. As he tightened the noose around Sacramento, there was little opposition, and most of the enemy forces simply chose to surrender, since they no longer had contact with their superiors. Altogether there were 55,000 Chinese soldiers who surrendered over the next two days. The Neutron Bomb had accomplished the task that it was designed to do.

The worst news came after entering the city. There were more than 5,000 American citizens who lay dead. This was far above the estimates made before the bomb was detonated. But there were more than 140,000 Chinese dead. Logistically it was a huge success, but was this the only choice that could have been made? The debate lasted many years.

March 28: After arranging a compound for the Chinese, General Hollister turned his troops toward Monterey. With the attack on China now in full swing, the General decided to allow the Air Force and the Army helicopters, to lead the attack, and then to offer the Chinese an opportunity to surrender. By day the fighter-bombers led the way, then at night the Stealth bombers and the four Shadow helicopters (from Alabama) attacked the Chinese with deadly results. After three days of steady bombing, the General sent in a couple of Hummers with white flags flying. They were met in San Jose with Chinese flying their own white flags. The battle was over. Also, the troops were informed about the surrender of China. There was a big spontaneous victory parade in San Jose. California had suffered grievously. San Diego, Los Angeles, San Francisco and Oakland were gone. Hoover Dam was gone. Travis Air Force Base, China Lake Naval Weapons Center, Edwards Air Force base, Camp Pendleton (Marine Corps), Marine Corps Air Ground Combat Center, Fort Irvin National Training Center, Fort Hunter, Camp Roberts, and Beale Air Force Base were all gone. Altogether California had lost about four million citizens and soldiers.

From the initial stages to the end, the Americans in California had lost more than 50,000 soldiers in battle, mostly from the National Guard. In addition to the losses from the nuclear bombs, the civilian toll was more than 100,000, including the 10,000 from Sacramento. Many civilians had put up a valiant fight. The Chinese dead were about 200,000, including the 140,000 dead in

Sacramento. Another 50,000 had been killed by our planes and helicopters in the Battle of Monterey (named that, although very little actual fighting took place in Monterey). Others were lost in various skirmishes from Monterey to Sacramento.

CHAPTER 26
TIME RUNS OUT

March 25: U.N. Headquarters in Geneva.

A meeting of the leaders of the allies took place in Geneva, Switzerland. All the leaders were present: President Oderon of the United States, Prime Minister Baker of Great Britain, President Du Jacque of France, Chancellor Schmidt of Germany, President Ferraz of Spain, President Ciampi of Italy, Prime Minister Jagon of Japan, Prime Minister George of Australia, Prime Minister Williams of Canada and Russia's President Kostar met in Geneva.

The subject was what to do with China, in light of continued resistance to disarmament and outside observation of the process. There is no record of what was stated by each representative, but at the end a decision was made:

1. Destroy China's nuclear arms and the factories which make them.

2. Destroy China's armies and munitions factories.
3. Do not bomb the cities and factories unless China continues to refuse to disarm.
4. Divide China into smaller countries, and return any occupied country to self government.

The leaders did not want to destroy China, but desired that the Chinese govern themselves and produce enough food and manufactured goods to maintain their own countries. Occupation by foreign troops was not seen as a good alternative, unless further negotiations with China failed.

March 28. With no more response from China, the plan was implemented.

Step one: For the central Nuclear plants, Russia sent in five missiles with thermonuclear warheads. These were followed by five American sub launched missiles with the same targets. This made sure that the underground facilities were destroyed.

Step two: Great Britain and France launched four ICBMs with MIRV[4] missiles at the primary military installations and troop concentrations. These would total sixteen thermonuclear warheads in all.

Step three: B-5 bombers from the U.S. launched three GBU-33 satellite guided missiles

---

[4]Multiple Intercontinental Reentry Vehicle

with three MIRV nuclear warheads (of the atomic bomb design) on each toward the munitions plants in China. These were smaller tactical nuclear bombs, aimed at particular plants. If these were intercepted, then a second bomber was in place to make a similar launch thirty minutes later. It was not needed.

At the end of the day all but one military target was annihilated. The army base near Kunming was left untouched. Apparently one of the sixteen missiles launched by France and Great Britain had failed to reach its target or had not detonated. A Russian sub launched a subsequent missile at the target early on March 29. It succeeded.

Now, China had received her retribution as she had dealt it out to the United States. Furthermore, she understood that the United States did not stand alone. If China had failed to surrender and disarm, then even more such actions were in store for her. However, with most of the army, air force and navy lying in ruins, all believed that China would now cooperate.

CHAPTER 27
NEGOTIATING TIME, MARCH 30

Ambassador Lucius Wentworth now sent an urgent appeal to the Chinese Government. Choung Waer (Taiwan), the Russian, French, and British ambassadors were contacted. At 9:25 a.m. Wentworth received a reply. It was curt but responsive, "Please meet with us at 11:00 a.m. today to continue talks."

All five men went together. Notably, Had Woang was not present, but Premier On was. Ambassador Wentworth wasted no time in explaining the allies' position. "What you have heard about the destruction of your country is all true. I have last minute photographs of your missile manufacturing plants, your nuclear facilities and a number of your military bases. In effect, they no longer exist. There are other missiles waiting to be launched if you refuse these terms of surrender. You will have twenty-four hours to consider your position. There will be no more negotiations.

First, China must disarm.

Second, Inspections of the disarmament by allied forces must be allowed.

Third, All territories occupied by China must be allowed to form their own government.

Fourth, China must be divided into two countries with distinct elected governments. Taiwan may be a part of whichever country she chooses. The exact nature of the division will be decided at a later date.

If China agrees to these terms, then no occupation force will be sent in to govern China. Failure to agree to these terms will mean more warfare and a full occupation of the country.

With that the ambassadors of the allies left without waiting for a reply.

March 31:

The Chinese leaders responded by 11:00 a.m. with the invitation for another meeting. All the allied ambassadors attended.

Premier On presided, "It seems that we have no choice but to capitulate. We do have one request. Please allow representatives from different areas of our country to make the decision on how to divide our country. Also, we will need some time to communicate this to our countrymen. We will begin by broadcasting the terms of this agreement to our country at 1:00

p.m. today. We will begin disarming immediately, but it would not be wise to throw all of our military out of work at once. Perhaps some of your military people could be put in charge of the individual units that are still standing. This would allow you to observe the disarmament and be in control of it. We await your timetable."

Thus, ended the most devastating war of all time.

The United States of America lost 101 million persons, most of the manufacturing capability and financial institutions, most of the military, all but three of the major cities, about half of the farmland due to radiation, and a myriad of long term health problems. But she helped bring about defeat for the aggressors. Also Cuba was invaded and defeated. A new government was installed. Venezuela was occupied for a short period of time.

Great Britain had nearly 100,000 casualties, and France more than 120,000 from the nuclear blasts from the missiles launched from the Chinese submarine.

China lost about 220 million persons, including more than 50 million military personnel. Also she lost her nuclear resources, the military manufacturing facilities, four major cities, several occupied countries, and her autocratic government. Although no formal occupation took place, there were a great number of inspectors, and two new countries: North China

and South China.
The world was never again the same.

Post Script:

Memorial Day, 20XX. President Oderon invited the following to the White House: Captain George Ware, Staff Sergeant Amoco Hooks, Lt. Lance Lopez and his bride Nandy, Joe and Rita Richardson, WO2 Fran "the Fox" Schmidt, Sgt. Louis Harris from Corpus Christie, MSgt Cory B. O'Reiley from Louisville, and Linda Baker from Redstone Arsenal, Alabama. They stood with all the other dignitaries.

President Oderon spoke," These are only a few of the people responsible for our continued existence as a nation. Many are no longer with us. Our country was attacked for only one reason: we stood in the way of a few people who wanted to rule the world. May it always be said that we will continue to stand in the way of anyone, anywhere who wants to do the same.

It will take many years to rebuild this great nation, but I have no doubt that we will rebuild as long as we have people like these standing here with me. Thank you all. We are proud to call you fellow Americans."

George Washington's prayer recorded in the Washington Monument:

"Almighty God; We make our earnest prayer that Thou wilt keep the United States in Thy holy protection; that Thou wilt incline the hearts of the citizens to cultivate a spirit of subordination and obedience to government; and entertain a brotherly affection and love for one another and for their fellow citizens of the United States at large.

And finally that Thou wilt most graciously be pleased to dispose us all to do justice, to love mercy, and to demean ourselves with that charity, humility, and pacific temper of mind which were the characteristics of the Divine Author of our blessed religion, and without a humble imitation of whose example in these things we can never hope to be a happy nation. Grant our supplication, we beseech Thee, through Jesus Christ our Lord.

Amen."

ADDENDUM
LIST OF CAHARACTERS

International Leaders:

Prime Minister Baker of Great Britain,
President Du Jacque of France,
Chancellor Schmidt of Germany,
President Ferraz of Spain,
President Ciampi of Italy,
Prime Minister Jagon of Japan,
Prime Minister George of Australia
Prime Minister Williams of Canada.
President Kostar of Russia
Tau Yua Premier of China (first)
Premier On of China (second)

American National Leaders:

President Jake Oderon
Vice President Lon Anderson
Director of Homeland Security John Taylor
(Retired General Marine Corps)
Col. Joe Mustedo, of the Air Force

157

(intelligence – satellites & Capt. Howie Holton)
    Secretary of State Joslyn Ohman
    Secretary of Defense Jack Peremba
    Chairman of the Armed Forces Admiral Kerry Eubanks
    Speaker of the House Joseph Lewis
    Minority Leader of the Senate Young Son
    Personal Advisor to the President, Julie Gonzalez

Ambassadors to China:

    Lucius Wentworth *ambassador to China*
    Colonel Harmon of the U.S. Army
    Ambassador Sterling (England
    Taiwan, Choung Waer

Iran & Springfield, Missouri:

    Joe and Rita Richardson, Adou Barak, Killen Dabou, Arn Salim (Captain)

Oregon:

    Captain George Ware of the National Guard
    Sergeant Williams, and Lance Corporal George

Battle of Mobile, Alabama:

    Maj. General H. C. Hamilton, commander of

the Alabama National Guard, and veteran of the Gulf Wars

WO1 Mel Hammond, WO2 Fran "the Fox" Schmidt, and WO1 Goal Washington

Shadow pilots in Ala.: WO3 Max Thackery and WO2 Joe Ballew helicopter pilots

WO1 Jo Ling, WO1 Suzy Mark, and WO1 Chuck Chissom copilots

Lt James Boyd led surveillance party into Mobile, Pfc. Sanders(wounded)

Israel:

Captain Matthew Goldberg took off in an X-10,

Major Solomon Williams , Lt. Yishtak Zeewi : pilots

Battle of Wilmington, Delaware:

Lt. General Max Hardin. (Ft. Dix, New Jersey)

Lt. Forrest Macon, Army from Ft. Dix

Amoco Hooks, Marshew (mother), Malene Dillard grandmother

Major Yarnell C.O. New Castle Guard

Mr. Amos Peabody, Civilian who aided Amoco

Lt. Jeff George pilot (N.Y.)

Explosives team: Middletown, Delaware: John Montesi, National Guard,, munitions

Elizabeth (Dardin) (wife), Sara, daughter S.Sgt.

Vance Wiley, Pfc. Tamara Ramage, and Pfc. Ralph Frank

Battle of Ft. Lauderdale, Florida:

Major Charles Harris Fla National Guard
Captain Lewis, and Lt. Jarvis led squad into Ft. Lauderdale

Battle of Corpus Christie, Texas

Retired Gen. Andrew Summers Texas
Petty Officer 2nd Class Jeff Baumer, Petty Officer 3rd Class James Gurley and Seaman Lance Lopez (Seals)

Sgt. Louis Harris survived in Corpus Christie

Battle of Louisville, Kentucky:

Governor Kile Willis (Kentucky)
Colonel Jacoby (commander)
Col. Howard
S.Sgt. Cory B. O'Reiley

Battle of Sacramento and Monterey, California:

Captain Ron Witherspoon (Air Force pilot, whose name was forever kept secret)
Colonel John Younis (Captain Witherspoon's commander)
General R.T. Hollister, commander of the California forces
Colonel Quentin Rodriguez, commander of

the forces engaged in the battle of Monterey

Cruise Ship:

Lewis and Naomi Smith

Submarine Personnel:

Captain Blake – Captain Finihas submarine captains

England:

Captain Richards of the RAF

Printed in the United Kingdom
by Lightning Source UK Ltd.
131535UK00001B/134/A